Stories Too Scary For Children

Jules Fox

SCARY

My one and a half year old daughter loves to run up to me in the morning and say "scary!"

She walks into the closet and "hides," even though her arms and legs are sticking out.

When she walks out, she wants me to say "Boo!"

I do it. She shakes and says "scary! More." Then she gets back into the closet.

Scary! More!

We all want to be scared sometimes.

It feels good.

Scary is exciting!

But we don't want to be too scared.

The stories in this book are meant to scare you and give you the shivers, but not nightmares.

If you find that after you read them, you can't sleep or that you wake up screaming, the stories might be too scary for you.

You could try sticking to the first few stories, as they are less scary. Or try reading in the daylight, maybe in mom and dad's lap.

Or if this book is way too scary, try putting it away and reading it when you are older.

I have put a Scare-ometer rating on each of these stories. They start at a one, which is like seeing a spider from far away. But they go all the way up to ten, which is like running through a graveyard at night with a zombie chasing you.

Whatever you do, do not read a ten on the Scare-ometer.

I wish you all good luck, and a good sleep tonight.

Mwa ha ha haaaaaaaaa.

- Jules

CONTENTS

HOW TO TELL SCARY STORIES

Some people have a hard time telling stories, especially funny or scary stories. There's an art to it, and it's not easy.

Storytelling doesn't come naturally to most of us, it's a skill we have to learn and develop.

Let me tell you a few secrets about how to do it well.

1. Atmosphere: dim the lights. Find a good scary place like the basement, the attic or outside.
2. Voice: moderate your voice when you tell a scary story. Start in a normal tone. Then get softer to build suspense. Save your loud voice for the scary part, after your listeners have been expecting your soft voice. Try to find funny elements to make your listeners laugh. This will catch them off guard when the story gets scary.
3. Noises: add in some good, scary noises. Not just at the end. Put a few sound effects all throughout and it will make a broad and believable world for your story to take place.
4. Truth: even if you are telling the craziest hog wild lie, stick to it. Give your listeners a nice, straight face like you are telling them the truth. This will add to the scary factor because people are naturally very trusting.
5. Practice: your stories will get better and better as you tell them more and more. Your listeners might want to hear the same story again and again. That's a good sign. Try practicing in front of a mirror, or to a group of imaginary friends, or even scarier, go to a graveyard and practice telling your story to dead people to see what they think.

You can also get the audiobook to accompany this collection of terrifying tales. See how I tell stories. You don't have to do it like me, every story can be told a million ways. But you might want to see what's possible so you can build your version of the story.

Good luck, and happy scary story telling. May the wind be at your back and the grave beneath your feet.

The Closet Kid

1
SCARE-OMETER

1 – THE CLOSET KID

Brandon ran into the closet and closed the door most of the way. He looked out the crack. Lynne was walking down the hall, getting closer and closer.

"Boo!" called Brandon and jumped out of the closet.

Lynne jumped up and shook. "Why are you always scaring me, B?"

"Don't call me B, L," said Brandon.

"I don't mind if you call me L," said Lynne. "Just stop scaring me. I can't walk by any of the closets in the house anymore without thinking that someone is going to jump out and yell at me."

Brandon smiled.

"Please," said Lynne. "I'm going to go sneak a popsicle. Do you want one?"

"Totally," said Brandon.

"Okay," said Lynne. "Could you please get out of the closet?"

Brandon stepped out of the closet.

"And close the door?" she said, walking down the hall.

"I'll be in the living room," called Brandon. "Thanks Lynne."

Brandon opened the closet door and snuck inside again. He laughed so hard he had to put his hand over his mouth.

He waited and waited. She was probably also making a peanut butter sandwich. Lynne ate about ten peanut butter sandwiches a day.

And she was wrapping the bottom of the popsicles in paper towel, for sure. Lynne was a neat freak. It might have been more scary to her that someone left the closet door open a crack, than that someone jumped out to say 'boo.'

Footsteps came down the hall, getting closer.

Brandon crouched, ready to pounce.

This was going to be hilarious.

Hopefully, Lynne was holding a glass of milk, and the sandwich and two popsicles. She was going to spill milk all over herself for sure.

Brandon put his hand back over his mouth. He could feel the laugh bubbling up and spoiling the surprise.

The door closed.

It was dark.

Brandon couldn't see anything.

"Brandon, I asked you to close that closet door!" Lynne shouted, outside.

Brandon reached up and grabbed the handle. He would jump out and scare her now!

But the handle wouldn't turn.

He twisted and pulled.

The door was locked from the outside!

It was really creepy in the closet. It smelled like old leather and sweaty gym shoes. Furry coats and long sleeves dangled like dead people's arms!

Brandon couldn't find a comfortable place to sit.

He shifted his weight, trying to cuddle into the sporting equipment all over the floor. But every time he moved, something dug into his ribs or poked his legs.

Oh man! What do you do?

The carpet in the closet blocked out the only light coming in from the hallway.

It was dark.

And scary.

Brandon reached up and grabbed the door handle again.

Strangely enough, it turned this time.

He pushed the door a crack.
He looked out the little crack of light.
The coast was clear.
Brandon pushed the door open a little more.
He put one foot out the door.
Brandon slipped into the hallway.
"Boo!" yelled Lynne.
Brandon jumped up in the air and screamed.
"Gotcha," she said. "Here's your popsicle."
Brandon was right.
The popsicles were wrapped in paper towel around the stick.
And she did have a peanut butter sandwich.

Dry Mouth

2
SCARE-OMETER

2 – DRY MOUTH

Abby stuck her yellow plastic shovel in the sand. "Beach day!" she shouted. She flipped sand up in the air.

"Yeah, beach day!" said her dad. He wiped sand from his face. "Be careful with that thing, Abby. You're getting sand everywhere."

Abby stopped shoveling. She took one big scoop and brought it up to her face. She looked back at her family.

Her mom shook her head 'no.'

Abby took a big bite of sand.

Her Grandma shook her finger in the air. "Don't eat too much sand, or it might dry you all up on the inside."

Abby took another big bite of sand and swallowed.

"Abby, it was cute when you were a little baby," said her mom. "But you're almost five now."

"I am little," said Abby. "And I am cute."

"Yes," agreed her mom. "You're very cute. And you're smaller than we are. But you are big enough and old enough to know that eating sand is icky. It's not good for you."

Abby's mom picked up a popsicle from the ice chest. She unwrapped it and handed it to Abby. "Here," she said. "Enjoy."

Abby grabbed the popsicle and shoveled sand onto it. Then she put the popsicle into her mouth and stared at her mom.

"There are sand crabs in there," said Abby's grandma. "You might eat one accidentally and it will pinch your tongue."

"You know what we do to little girls who don't

listen?" her dad asked. He ran over to Abby and kissed her shoulders, tickling her. He started digging up huge handfuls of sand.

Abby laughed and kicked playfully at her dad.

Soon, a big pit revealed dark wet sand beneath and light beige sand on top. Abby's dad picked Abby up and plopped her into the pit. Then he buried her.

Abby lay there, letting the sand pile on top of her.

Her dad pushed even more over her belly so that a large lumpy sandcastle was on top. He put a stick into the tip of the hill and then a leaf on the stick. "There," he said. "I now claim this beach to be Abby beach. Now, can you get out?"

Abby squirmed. She tried to kick her feet. They were stuck. She tried to move her arms. They were pinned down by the weight of the sand.

Abby tried twisting back and forth but she could not move from the neck down.

"At least that will keep you from eating sand," said her mom.

Abby craned her neck up and pushed her mouth forward. She took a big bite of sand and swallowed.

"Just ignore her," said Abby's grandma.

Abby took another bite of sand. She choked it down. "This sand is delicious, Mom. Mmmmmm." She took another mouthful.

Abby's mom and dad looked at each other.

Her dad shrugged his shoulders.

Her mom shook her head. She stood up and walked to the water. "I'm going for a quick dip."

Abby's throat stung. The sand scraped her when she swallowed, like rough sandpaper on the inside of her mouth and down to her tummy.

It hurt to take breaths of the warm, salty beach air. She tried breathing through her nose.

The waves crashed on the shore. So much water,

and so close!

Abby had to go pee. She opened her mouth to tell her grandma, but no sound came out.

Abby tried to swallow. She had no saliva left.

She tried to cough, but it hurt too bad.

Abby tried to wriggle out of the sand, but it was too heavy and she was too small and weak.

She let go and her pee came out, warm and wet. It soaked her and the sand around her. Now she was stuck buried in the sand and her pee.

Abby started to cry, but no tears came out.

Maybe she could eat her way out!

Abby spooned some sand with her tongue and tried to push it away from her face. It rolled into her mouth, coating her teeth.

She tried to spit out the sand, but the harder she struggled, the more she swallowed.

Abby tried looking behind her. Her grandma was sitting in a beach chair holding a book. Her head was tipping forward as she nodded off to sleep and woke herself up.

Her dad was laid out on the beach, tanning his hairy chest. It looked like a poodle was laying on top of him.

Her mom was walking back from the ocean, wringing out her hair.

Abby's mom looked around their area. "Where's Abby?" she asked.

"What?" asked her dad. "Isn't she right over..." he rolled over and looked at where Abby lay buried.

Abby's mom ran over to Abby and dug into the sand castle.

Abby tried to speak, but her mouth was too dry. She looked up into her mom's eyes.

"She's not here," her mom called. She looked down right at Abby, digging through the sand. She dug through

Abby, deep into the watery sand. Her voice was wavering. "Where did she go?"

Abby tried to tell her mom she was there. She was there watching her. She could not say a thing.

Abby's grandma shrugged her shoulders. "She was here a minute ago," she said. "I was sitting here the whole time. I didn't see her move."

Abby's mom called out, "Abby! Abby! Abby where are you?" She ran up and down the beach.

Abby's dad ran over to the sand pit and kept digging. He dug left and right. Somehow, he could not see Abby.

The lifeguard came over and joined the commotion, and soon, the police arrived. They all searched until the sun set, but nobody could find Abby.

They gave up the search and the crowd went home.

Her mom stood crying on her dad's shoulder for hours, while Grandma rubbed their backs.

'But I'm right here!' thought Abby. She couldn't speak. Now she couldn't turn her head either. She just looked up at the sky.

Eventually, her family packed up and went home.

Sand crabs crawled sideways and looked down at Abby. They carried little specks of her to the water.

Finally, she was wet again!

Abby drifted into the crashing waves and sank to the ocean floor, swept out to sea, spinning, spinning, spinning.

3 – GRANDPA'S GHOST

Sam pushed up to her tiptoes, her little fingers curled over the polished wood. Her eyes barely made it over the rim.

Grandpa's face was close enough to touch, if she extended her finger. His eyes were closed. He lay back in the casket like it was comfortable. His wrinkly skin finally had a chance to rest. It had been trying so hard to stay up.

What would happen if Sam pulled Grandpa's eyes open? Were they gone? Or do they keep looking at the back of your eyelids after you die?

It was the first dead person she had seen. And now here he was in their entryway, mostly blocking the staircase.

His moustache whiskers didn't even wiggle when he breathed in and out. *Oh yeah, because he wasn't breathing in and out any more.*

Sam dropped her teddy bear over the edge of the coffin. It rolled a bit and ended up face down near Grandpa's armpit.

Her mom picked it up and looked down at her. "No, sweetie. That's really kind of you though." She offered Sam the bear.

Sam took it and dropped it back into the coffin. "Who's Grandpa going to snuggle with?" she asked.

Her mom smiled warmly, trying to hold back tears. "With Grandma." Her voice broke. She reached for the bear again.

Sam squinched up her face. "You don't think Grandma's going to be mad that he got married again to my fake Grandma?"

Her mom thought about it for a moment. "She's your Grandma in law, sweetie. You can just call her

Verna."

Sam shrugged her shoulders. "And then who is fake Grandma going to snuggle with when she goes to Heaven?"

Dad tried to suppress a laugh, but it came out louder than expected. "Fake Grandma's not going to heaven, Sam."

Mom elbowed him, hard.

Dad laughed again, but he kept his mouth closed this time.

"You're right," she said to Sam. She snuggled the Teddy bear up to Grandpa's face. "You have always been a dear heart. I know this bear means a lot to you."

Sam hugged her mom. "Grandpa meant a lot to me, too."

Dad wrapped his arms around them both. "I think we could all use some sleep, girls. Let's all go upstairs and brush teeth before fake Grandma comes in and stinks this place up with her lousy perfume."

*

Sam tossed and turned. She rolled over onto something fuzzy. She reached up to touch it.

It was bear!

She opened her eyes.

The room was dark.

Something was in her chair. Maybe just a shadow.

"I didn't want to freak you out, kid." Grandpa stood up and walked slowly towards the bed. "It's your bear. But your mom's right, you have always been a dear heart."

Sam's heart raced.

She looked up at the shadow getting closer. "But you're dead, Grandpa," she said. "You can't keep walking around.

"Don't worry," said Grandpa. "We get a few extra days to sort things out. They put me in the ground tomorrow morning."

He kneeled down by the bedside. The dim light coming in through the window illuminated his features.

He was a kind man with a warm smile like mom. His eyes twinkled, even when he was dead.

"We still have a few hours, let's go!" he chuckled softly.

Sam sat up in bed. "We?"

"I can't drive," said Grandpa. "After my brain popped I don't move so well here." He tried to lift one arm, but it wouldn't go. He lifted the other arm and pointed in that general direction.

"I can't drive either, Grandpa," said Sam. "I'm only eleven!"

"Nonsense," said Grandpa. "When I was your age, if you could see over the wheel, you could drive. Now let's go paint the town red!"

Sam got out of bed and put slippers on. "I don't think we have red paint."

Grandpa laughed. "It's an expression! It means let's go have some fun."

They snuck down the stairs and out the door.

Sam eyed his coffin as they passed it. It seemed strange all empty and wrinkled. She could smell fake Grandma's stinky perfume on the way out the door.

They got into the car.

Sam couldn't see over the steering wheel. But she could see through the space between the dashboard and the top of the wheel.

"Alright," said Grandpa. "First stop, my old neighbor Mrs. Jenkins." He sat back in the seat.

They didn't move.

Sam looked at Grandpa's seat belt. It was not fastened. She cleared her throat.

Grandpa looked down at his seat belt. He looked up at Sam. "I'm already dead!" he said. "You know in my day, we didn't even have seat belts."

Sam stared him down.

"Okay, okay," Grandpa buckled his belt. "You drive a hard bargain."

Sam started the car.

She revved the engine.

She adjusted the rearview mirror.

She reversed slowly down the driveway, turning the handle carefully when they got to the street.

Sam put it in drive and gassed the car. It jumped and sped forward, jerking this way and that as she steered the wheel trying to slow it down.

"Now this is a ride!" Grandpa rolled down the window and put his arm out.

Sam slowed the car a bit and straightened out. "This isn't that hard once you get the hang of it," she said.

They drove right next to Grandpa's house.

"Okay," said Grandpa. "You wait in the car. I'll be right back."

He went limping up the wet sidewalk to his neighbors' house. When he got up to the front step, he dinged the bell and came limp running back to the car. He ducked down and snuck back inside.

Mrs. Jenkins opened the front door. She looked mad. "Who in God's name is ringing my bell at two in the morning?" she yelled.

Grandpa laughed. "I owed her one," he whispered. "Now let's get out of here!"

Sam hit the gas.

The car lurched forward at an angle and smashed into a parked car.

Sam opened her eyes wide.

"Better let me try," said Grandpa.

Sam unbuckled and hopped into the back seat.

Grandpa pulled his legs up and shifted over to the driver's seat.

"Marvin?" Mrs. Jenkins shouted to them. "Is that you? Well you better get back into the ground, you're supposed to be dead."

Grandpa laughed harder. He sped off down the street, skidding into about every parked car on the way back home.

Sam sat in the middle of the back seat. She was buckled up, but she reached her hands out and grabbed onto both door handles too. "Grandpa," she said. "Why didn't you want to see fake Grandma?"

Grandpa looked up into the rearview mirror to meet her eyes. "The only woman I ever loved is your real Grandma. I just got lonely, I guess. After she was gone, and you were at school and your mom and dad had work to do. It's real lonely being old. I hope someday you meet someone who wants to be with you for a long, long time."

They were quiet the rest of the way home.

With the side mirrors hanging off and busted headlight, Grandpa pulled the car onto the lawn. He pulled a pipe out of his jacket pocket and placed the tip in his mouth.

"Not much time left," he said. "One more whiskey drink, and I will be off to bed."

"One more?" Sam asked. "How much..."

"Could you find your Grandpa a match, sweetie?" Grandpa left the broken car in the yard and wandered into the house, with Sam right behind him.

He fiddled with the pipe in his mouth, patting down his jacket pockets, then his pants pockets.

He went to the kitchen and took down a bottle of mom's whiskey.

He took a big glug.

"Wish she could join me," he said. "Tell your mama

she has great taste in whiskey. Always has." He put his hand into a fist and raised it into the air. "One, Hi, Ho!"

He spilled a good portion onto the floor and then the carpet trying to get the cap back on. He made it back to the entryway and climbed into his coffin. "You mind locking me into this bed of nails? Took me long enough to get out."

Sam nodded and closed the lid.

Just before it shut, Grandpa held the top. "Wait," he said. "I would have given you a hug, but..."

"I understand," said Sam.

"You know I love you," said Grandpa. "Now go have a good life. I'll be cheering for you from wherever I end up."

Samantha closed the lid and locked it.

She heard Grandpa strike a match inside the coffin.

She ran up to bed and fell into a deep sleep.

*

"SAM!" her father shouted.

The door to her room opened and he and her mom walked in.

"Sweetie," said her mom.

"No," her dad was gruff. "Sometimes you have to act like a parent, Fran."

Her mom sighed. "You don't know that any of this was her," she whispered to dad.

Dad put up his index finger for silence. "Why is our smashed up car in the middle of the yard?" he asked. "And why does it smell like alcohol down in the kitchen and living room? And where is my hand carved pipe?"

"Sweetie," said mom, sweetly. "Are you having a hard time because Grandpa passed?"

Sam sat up in bed.

She was still tired.

She looked at her dad, then her mom.

"Grandpa says you have great taste in whiskey," said Sam. "He took your bottle with. I guess he didn't want the bear after all."

Mom and dad stared at Sam.

Sam held the bear in one hand. She curled the other hand into a fist and lifted it into the air. "One, Hi, Ho!" she smiled.

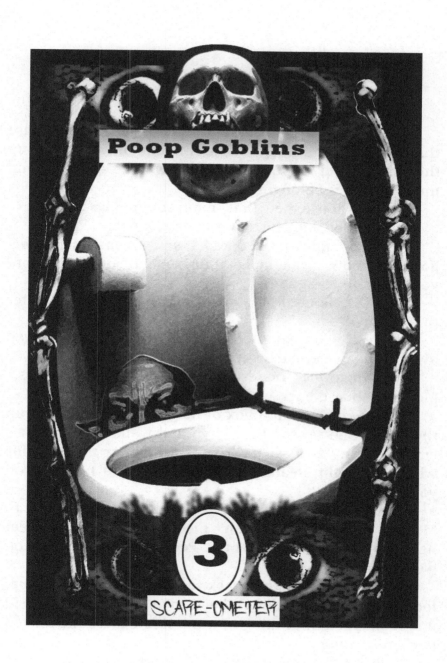

Poop Goblins

3

SCARE-OMETER

4 – POOP GOBLINS

On a windy drive up a steep hill was a new house that looked over a sleepy town. A family of two picked up their boxes and moved in. They swept the cobwebs and unpacked their belongings.

"New house, new life!" mom shouted up the stairs.

"No life!" Melissa shouted back down.

"I like houses!" shouted mom. "It makes me feel good to know I can make things nice. Don't you want your mom to feel good?"

"NO!" shouted Melissa. "Don't want your daughter to feel good?"

"Yes!" mom shouted back. "That's why we moved away from all those dangerous friends of yours."

"Dangerous friends are better than no friends," Melissa shouted back.

Mom picked up a box of magazines and walked up the stairs. She set the box down and walked to Melissa's empty room. "At least no friends are better than friends who get caught stealing from the mall and blame it on you."

Her mom came in and sat on the bare floor next to Melissa. "Honey, those aren't nice friends. You can meet new people here. Good people. People who will treat you well."

Melissa turned her back to her mom and stood up, looking out the window. She leaned on the windowsill and it snapped off, falling in front of her toes. She looked back at her mom.

"It's a fixer upper," said her mom. "There are some broken bits, but we can make it look great! Then we can sell it and move wherever you would like to move."

"Can we move back in with dad?" asked Melissa.

"Except there," said her mom. She leaned in for a hug.

"No," Melissa pushed her mom away. "You can't just hug me and make everything okay. I'm not five."

Her mom held her arms open. "You're still my baby girl. And you're not even a teenager yet."

"I almost have boobs," Melissa said.

"That doesn't make you an adult," said her mom. She sighed. "Why don't I go unpack some more stuff while you sit here and mope."

Melissa stomped the ground. "I'm not moping," she said to the floor.

"Okay, then you can sit here and not mope," said her mom. She got up and walked out of the room. In a moment she was banging boxes around downstairs.

Melissa picked up the windowsill. This house was old. And creaky. You could see the whole town from her room, up on the second floor of their house on the hill.

Why were adults so dumb?

Mom kept moving and moving like the houses were going to make her happy. She only pretended to be happy.

Melissa walked over and closed her door. The bottom hinge squeaked with strain, then popped. The door slid sideways until the top hinge caught it, slamming the bottom into the wood.

"Sweetie?" mom called. "Be careful with the house while we're fixing it.

Melissa wasn't fixing anything.

She walked back to the middle of the room and spread out a blanket. She took out one of her textbooks from her last school. She had forgotten to return it.

It was about animals and how they adapted to their environment.

Her eyes drooped. Her head dropped.

21

When she awoke, it was dark.

Something was dragging across the floor.

"Mom?"

No answer.

Melissa stood up and ran her hand along the broken door, following the frame up until it clicked the light switch on.

She covered her eyes as the bare bulb pierced through the night.

Something dragged again. Light. Wood? A box?

"Hey, mom?" Melissa raised her voice. She opened the door.

Light flooded the hallway.

Melissa fumbled in the dark for a hallway light switch.

She clicked it on and off.

Nothing.

"Figures," she said.

She squinted her eyes. Too hard to tell in the dark.

Why was her mom in the dark?

Whatever, mom was weird. Mom is weird. Mom will always be weird.

Melissa went back to sleep.

*

"Sorry I left a stink bomb in there last night," her mom leaned in for a hug, catching Melissa's shoulder.

"What?" Melissa shrugged off the hug.

"A poop," mom said. "I didn't realize the flush wasn't working. I'll get somebody to come and fix it today."

"But there wasn't a poop in there this morning," Melissa looked at her mom curiously.

Her mom shrugged and smiled. "Maybe it flushes itself! I don't know. What do you want for breakfast?"

Melissa started walking downstairs. "Is that a real question, or are we just going to eat cereal?"

"I could make pancakes," her mom said. "I just need to find the pots and pans. And the mix. I could go buy mix! Oh but I think the movers have the pots and pans."

In the kitchen, Melissa poured a bowl of cereal. She looked in the fridge.

No milk.

Today was going to suck.

She crunched on dry corn flakes.

The movers didn't come all day.

No boxes equals no bed.

Mom went about her batty business of unpacking and then repacking the same items. She dragged boxes around, not sure of where to put anything because the house was so bare.

By sunset, it was messier than yesterday with less stuff unpacked.

Melissa lay down on her sheets again, in the middle of her room. The floor was surprisingly comfortable.

Mom knocked on the door. "Hey, sweetie." She walked in without waiting for an answer. "Sorry I keep having to poop at night. I tried dumping water down the drain but it won't go."

Melissa ignored her, reading a magazine article about how to twirl her eyelashes.

Her mom picked up another sheet and laid it over Melissa. "You can go on top of mine and I'll figure it out in the morning."

Melissa put the magazine over her face. "Mom, that's disgusting." She laughed. "I'll just go poop in here, it will be an improvement."

No response. Melissa took the magazine off of her face.

Mom was crying.

"I'm joking," Melissa said. "This house is going to be great."

"I'm trying," said Mom. She held her nose up and tried to walk out of the room without tears falling to the floor. She ended up scuffling with the door, trying to get it open, then trying harder to get it closed.

The top hinge came off the door and the whole thing fell inwards, slamming on the ground.

Mom laughed.

Melissa laughed.

"Goodnight," mom said. She walked into the hall, disappearing in the dark.

"Goodnight, mom!" Melissa said. "Hey, we really need to get a hallway light!"

"We have one, sweetie!" mom said. She flicked a switch and a light came on for a moment, then burnt out and a sparks showered down from the ceiling.

Mom sighed and walked to her bedroom.

Melissa laid her head down and pretended to sleep. She held onto a flashlight underneath her sheets.

She resisted the urge to sleep.

Something was weird about the house. Mom bought it for really cheap. And yes, it needed a lot of work. But last night, the toilet didn't flush itself because Melissa would have heard it.

After about a half an hour, Melissa heard little footsteps coming down the hall. Then, another pair of footsteps followed a moment later.

Bingo.

Melissa pulled off her covers and walked to her doorway.

The footsteps were headed toward the bathroom.

Melissa put her finger over the flashlight button.

Not yet.

She followed the footsteps to the bathroom.

Something climbed up onto the toilet.

Melissa lifted the flashlight up.

Not yet.

Whatever was there snarled and snapped.

Click.

Melissa turned on the flashlight.

A little blue, bald man crouched on the toilet seat, holding mom's poop in one hand. He was dressed in animal fur, his other hand sticking out of his cloak to hold off the other man who looked very similar.

The other little blue, bald man stood on his tippy toes, grabbing at the poop.

They were both frozen, staring at the light. Their little beady eyes glowed red.

"MOM!" Melissa screamed.

Both men shivered and hopped when she spoke. The one on top of the toilet seat took a big bite of the poop in his hand.

The other man pulled him down and punched him in the tummy. He grabbed the other half of the poop and ate it.

Melissa felt sick. She tried to hold the flashlight steady but her hand shook. The light wobbled around the room.

"What happened?" mom walked into the hall, tying a robe around her.

The two little blue men dashed into the dark hall, past Melissa and mom.

"Oh my goodness, are they rats?" mom hugged Melissa.

Melissa hugged mom back. With her other hand, she shined her flashlight down the hall.

The backs of the bald heads of the little blue men could be seen, squeezing into the air duct.

"Oh boy," mom said. "I'll fix that in the morning."

Sprout

3

SCARE-OMETER

5 – SPROUT

Erik sat under the overhanging kitchen counter, eating an apple.

His mom popped her head under the edge. "Hey, buddy. What are you doing down here?"

Erik stopped eating and looked at his mom. He was quiet. He rested his teeth on the red skin for his next bite. He could smell the sweet inside.

"You can eat an apple," said his mom. "Dinner's not for another hour or so."

Erik stared at her.

"What?" asked his mom. "You're not eating apple seeds again, are you?"

Erik pulled the apple away and held it under his armpit.

"Don't ignore me, please," said his mom. She reached her hand out. "It's called stone walling when you don't say anything back. It doesn't feel good to mommy."

Erik kicked at his mom's hand.

His mom pulled her hand away, then reached out again. "Erik, you're almost thirteen years old. Sometimes you act like you're three!"

Erik spit at his mom.

"What did I do wrong?" his mom asked. She pulled her head back and left Erik sitting there. "I never dropped you or fed you paint chips. And you want to sit all alone and ignore me and eat apple seeds. Why? Because I asked you not to. I told you if you swallow those seeds, an apple tree is going to grow out of your stomach."

Erik's mom opened the fridge and pulled something out, slamming it down on the counter.

Erik ate the rest of his apple. He ate the core, seeds and all. He wiggled the hard stem between his fingers. Then he ate that too.

It was hard to swallow.

Erik crawled to the doorway.

He slid the screen sideways and crawled outside.

Sometimes he just liked rolling.

He lay down flat on the concrete and rolled to the edge, then down the stairs and into the yard.

The bumps didn't hurt that bad when you got used to it.

Erik decided to wriggle on his back across the grass.

Sometimes dirt goes up your shirt when you do that. But dirt isn't that bad.

Erik wriggled and rolled. Kind of like a dog. And why not? All dogs do is sit around having fun all day.

But not moms.

Moms sit around telling you what you should and shouldn't do all day, like bossing you around and watching everything you do is their life.

Erik screeched as a sharp pain stabbed his foot.

Something bit him!

He stopped wriggling and stood up.

But when he put weight down on his foot, it was a hundred times worse!

Erik fell back onto his butt.

He reached for his hurt foot and pulled the shoe off.

Something sharp was sticking out of his sock!

He looked at his shoe again. It wasn't a nail.

It was a worm!

Erik reached for the worm and touched it.

It was hard!

What the heck was a hard worm doing in his sock? Biting him?

Erik pulled the sock off. It was stuck right where the worm was, but he pulled as hard as he could and tore the fabric.

It hurt really bad.

The worm was inside his foot. But it wasn't moving.

He touched it again.

It wasn't a worm after all.

It was long and hard and twisty and pointy.

It was a root!

Erik didn't remember stepping on a root.

Another shooting pain came from his hand this time.

A root was wriggling out of his hand.

Erik pulled at that root with his other hand.

This one was bigger and it hurt too bad to touch.

He shook his hand as hard as he could, flapping it in the air.

Another pain stabbed his stomach and another in his butt cheeks at the same time.

No way. Was this really happening?

Erik tried to stand up, but he was stuck. The roots from his butt and one of the roots from his foot were digging into the ground.

He opened his mouth to yell, but no sound came out. Instead, a few roots popped out over his tongue and across his teeth, hanging like a mouthful of unchewed spaghetti.

He tried screaming again but the roots only came out further.

Erik watched in wide-eyed horror as the roots slipped down to the ground and planted his face into the dirt.

All he could see was an ant crawling under his nose and up his new roots, into his mouth.

He felt his body contort as the other roots took hold. Something was sprouting out of his back now.

Everything hurt. He couldn't move any of his muscles anymore. It was like they were all tied together.

An hour or so later, his mom came outside.

"Erik, time for dinner." She walked over to the new tree in the yard. "What in the..." she put her hand on the trunk and felt the fresh bark.

Erik couldn't see his mom, but he could hear her.

"These weeds grow so fast in summer," she said. "Better call the lawn care guys tomorrow."

She walked away.

"Erik?" she called. "Don't make our dinner get cold. I know you're out here somewhere."

The Crimson Pearl

3

SCARE-OMETER

6 – THE CRIMSON PEARL

Gani and her brother Tallai lived in a little grass hut, on a little sand dune, over a little beach, at the edge of a little village, on a little island.

Gani was tall for ten years old, a skinny girl that ate anything easy to prepare: bananas, coconuts, mangoes and oranges. When she was finished gathering fruit for her family for the day, she would usually rub her belly in the sunshine and take a long nap until dinner.

Tallai was broad, with a tummy as round as a breadfruit, but he would wait until after his sister and mother had eaten to touch the food. Each day he would plunge into the clear blue sea to gather shrimp, clams or a lucky lobster. If he managed to pry a rare pearl, he could trade it at the market for a sack of rice.

Every morning, their mother would place her open palm on each of their heads, then put her finger in her mouth and smear a little saliva in a line from their widow's peaks to their brows. She would say "beware the Grindylusca. They stole your father and they will try to take you, too!"

Gani would laugh and reply "Nanay, there is no such thing as Grindylusca. Father will return with the fortune he has made while he has been away. He never said goodbye."

Tallai would sigh. It had been years since the day their father had gone fishing in his kayak, but never returned.

One afternoon, Gani joined Tallai at the shore. She picked up a flat piece of coral and skipped it into the knee high waves. "I wish the ocean floor were covered in pearls, so we would never have to work again," she said.

Tallai smiled. "But I love diving," he replied. "I hope we find some big shrimp today, so Nanay can make ginataang sugpo." He and his sister put their coconut fiber diving bags over their shoulders.

Something twinkled deep below the surface of the water. "What's that?" asked Gani, stepping up to her ankles in the warm break.

Tallai shrugged his shoulders and joined his sister in the water. Sparkles shone through the ripples.

Gani took a deep breath and dove in, paddling easily down the slope. She opened her eyes and beheld a hundred pearls glistening in the shallows trailing to the ledge that dropped off a thousand span into darkness.

Tallai swam ahead of her, plucking a pearl from the sand, then surfacing.

Gani kicked hard and grabbed one of her own, then rose to the top, popping up through the waves and breathing in again.

Tallai tread water and held up his hand, plunking wet sand into the sea. "It's gone! I must have dropped it," he called to his sister.

Gani opened her clenched fist carefully, but found only sand and seawater. "I think I dropped mine too!" she exclaimed. "No worry, there are more than we can carry." She ducked under a wave and splashed back down, Tallai right behind her.

Past the coral and kelp beds, at the sandy bottom, Gani sifted a pearl through the sand and shoved it into her pouch, then another and another.

Tallai joined her, diving even deeper. He discovered a pink pearl the size of his fingernail. He popped it into his bag.

Not to be outdone, Gani plugged her nose and cleared her ears, pushing her way down the ocean ridge. The pearls grew larger and shinier the deeper they went.

Gani snatched a blue pearl the size of a lychee, then a dark purple one the size of her palm. She put handfuls of the precious gems into her pouch, pulling the straps tighter as the heavy load tugged her back.

Tallai paddled to Gani, blowing bubbles so he could sink. He waved to his sister and caught her eye, then pointed to the surface.

Gani nodded her head and Tallai pushed hard off the bottom, speeding up twenty feet to the surface. He popped out of the water, sucking in breath. He lay on his back and tread water.

At the floor, Gani saw a crimson pearl the size of her head, balanced on the edge of the rocky precipice. She swam toward it, blowing the last of her bubbles. Even in the water, the weight of the great stone pulled her down. As she turned the smooth surface in her hands, she saw that the opposite side of the pearl had a face made of bone, with black, hollow eye sockets looking back at her!

At the surface, Tallai looked into his bag. It was filled with sand and saltwater. He looked around, but Gani was nowhere to be found. He scanned across the seabed below him, but he did not see her there, either. He yanked off his bag and dove down deep to where they had been swimming.

The pearls were all gone.

Gani was not under the sea. She had vanished, along with her bag of pearls.

Tallai searched until the light in the sky grew dim. His arms and legs ached, his head spinning. He swam back to shore and belched up saltwater, coughing and spluttering.

With a heavy heart, Tallai walked back to his hut to tell his mother that Gani had disappeared. He wrapped up in her arms and cried quietly long into the night.

Over the years following, when there was no moon out and the clouds covered the stars, Tallai would spot a glowing crimson red from deep in the sea, and all around it, little flickers of the pearls lying on the bottom.

Surprise

4

SCARE-OMETER

7 – SURPRISE

"Not yet," Tammy pushed the cushions back on top of the two young boys, sandwiching them inside the couch.

She pushed a woman's head down behind the bushy plant.

"Uncle Albert, lose the shoes!" Tammy ran over and pulled Albert's shoes off. Steam came out of the holes on his socks. Or maybe it was the visible smell, wafting up.

"And where is Uncle Edward?" Tammy asked. "He's Grandma's first born son, you would think he could show up on her birthday. Goodness sakes."

She ran back to the table and picked up two presents. "Who left presents on the table? That will spoil everything we're working for here." She ran to the kitchen and put the presents on the counter.

Tammy ran back in to the living room. She could still see shoulders and ears and hands sticking out. "Guys, what is going on in here? I can see you all in your hiding places. Did none of you learn to play hide and seek when you were kids? We have one 80th birthday for Grandma and that is the oldest anyone in this family has lived to be. We all have a history of heart disease. Most of your parents and grandparents never made it past fifty." She shook her finger at everyone in the room.

"Today is a very special day," she added. "I mean I'm glad you could all make it out. But that doesn't excuse this!" she slapped Aunt Bertha's arm hanging over the chair.

Bertha yanked her arm back.

"Or this!" Tammy smacked an ear. Whomever it

38

was pulled their head behind the corner.

"And not this!" Tammy stomped on a foot sticking out.

Uncle Filbert pulled his foot up into his lap. "Oww, Tammy that's my broken toe. Now I have to go back to the hospital to get it set."

"You can go to the hospital later," Tammy barked.

"I need to pee," called one of the kids from somewhere.

"Then pee in your pants and we'll clean it up afterwards," Tammy called back. "Nobody is going to ruin this surprise."

She ran across the room and dimmed the light.

A little bang came from outside. Someone was coming.

"Okay, everyone, this is it!" Tammy whispered. She crept to the stairs and climbed quickly, hiding behind the railing. Then she changed her mind and tiptoed down as fast as she could, sliding in her socks across the floor until she wooshed into the kitchen.

The door opened.

Clomp.

Clomp.

Clomp.

The four metal legs of a walker appeared.

Clomp.

Clomp.

Clomp.

An old woman appeared.

Clomp.

Clomp.

Clomp.

She turned on the light. It was still dim.

Clomp.

Clomp.

Clomp.

Tammy walked out of the kitchen. She came toward Grandma with her arms open. "Oh, Grandma, I almost forgot what day it was. It's your…"

Grandma knocked her walker to the side. "Eat!" she said in a deep voice. She lunged at Tammy and sank her teeth into Tammy's shoulder.

Tammy screamed, clutching the deep wound on her shoulder. A big piece was missing.

Grandma munched and munched, catching the juice with her hand.

"Surprise!" everyone shouted in unison. They jumped out from behind the curtains, the plants, between the couch cushions, behind the couch, under the table, out of the bathroom and up the stairs.

Grandma wiped blood from her mouth.

"What's grandma doing?" asked a young boy. He took off his blue party hat.

"Help!" cried Tammy, backing away.

"She needs help," said Uncle Filbert. "Jimmy go help her, she's bleeding!"

Jimmy walked towards grandma. "Are you okay, Granny?" he pointed toward her mouth.

"Eat!" Grandma said in a very deep voice. She chomped off Jimmy's hand.

Jimmy looked at his wrist where the hand was missing. He screamed.

The room broke into a panic. Some people scrambled to help bandage Jimmy, and some people helped bandage Tammy. Others tried to hold Grandma down. They pinned her to the ground.

All Grandma could say was "Eat!" in some far away demon voice. She was incredibly strong for her old age. She left a few marks on Uncle Albert.

They stuffed socks in her mouth.

Then, the front door opened.

Uncle Edward walked in. Tears stained his cheeks.

"I'm sorry I missed the surprise party," he said. "Grandma died this morning. I drove her to the morgue. I didn't have the heart to call any of you."

"Whoa," said Uncle Edward. "Are you okay, Tammy? You look a little pale."

Tammy stumbled toward Uncle Edward. She opened her arms.

Uncle Edward opened his arms to hug her.

"Eat," said Tammy in a low voice.

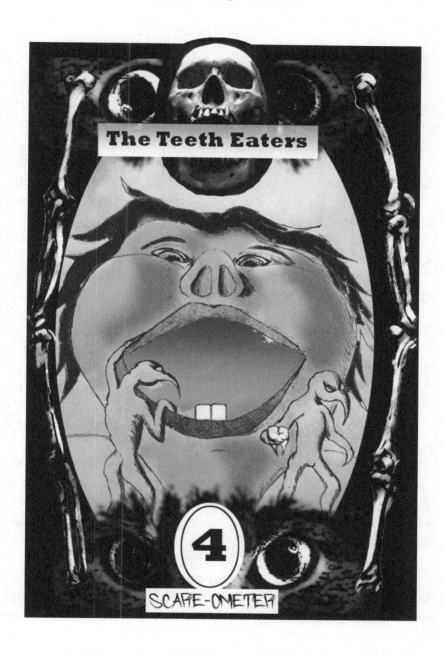

8 – THE TEETH EATERS

Barry opened the toothpaste and squeezed it. Three colors of gel squirted out. He licked the opening and rubbed the toothpaste onto his bottom two front teeth. Then he swallowed the paste.

Barry reached up and turned off the water in the sink. He hopped off his stool and snuck into his bedroom.

"Knock, knock!" his mom smiled at the open door. "Did you brush your teeth yet?"

"Yes!" Barry pulled his blankets up to his eyes. He squeezed his stuffed hippopotamus close to his cheek.

His mom sat down at the edge of his bed. "Let me smell."

Barry shook his head.

His mom moved in closer.

Barry kicked inside the blankets and laughed. "No!"

His mom pulled the blankets down and leaned in, way too close. She pinched his nose closed.

Barry tried to hold his breath. He had to breathe out.

His mom leaned in and smelled his breath. "You did brush, after all. Why do you hate brushing your teeth? If you don't brush them, these little teeth eater monsters will come and eat them up!" she popped a finger into his mouth and poked his tooth.

Barry pulled away. "No they won't mama."

"That's right," his mom said. "No they won't because you're going to brush them every morning and every night without fighting me on it and making me smell your breath."

She hugged Barry. "I love you. Sweet dreams."

He hugged her back. "You're okay mama."

She pulled back and stared at him, smiling. "Okay?

Okay!? I'll show you just okay." She leaned in and tickled him until he farted. "Okay," she said and patted his head.

Barry laughed and pulled the blankets up tight.

His mom got up and shut the lights off, blew him a kiss and shut the door. "Pew!" she called through the door. "That one blasted all the way into the hallway!" Her footsteps echoed down the hall.

Barry closed his eyes and smiled. He sniffed the air. "That's a real stinker!"

He lifted up his blanket and tried to fan the air.

The blanket settled down on him, soft and cozy.

Barry yawned. The mint smell was gone. His breath was stinky too.

He put one finger up on his teeth and wiggled it around. A little slippery slime came off.

He touched his tooth in the far back. Little raised up bumps rubbed his finger.

"Eww," he pulled his finger out and wiped it off on the blanket.

He closed his eyes and rolled over, giving one more yawn before he fell fast asleep.

Skrt, skrt, skrt.

Barry opened his eyes. It was dark. Super duper middle of the night dark.

Skrt, skrt, skrt.

He popped up out of his warm blankets. The air was cool.

He looked around, but it was too dark to see anything.

Skrt, skrt, skrt.

Something was scratching at the door.

Barry leaned over and grabbed his Zoombla! action figure off the nightstand. He popped the head in and it glowed an eerie green. He pointed it at the door.

Too hard to tell.

Barry moved to the edge of the bed. He reached the

toy as far as his arms could go.

Still too hard to tell.

Barry set one toe on the ground. It was cold.

He lifted his toe back up.

The scratching was gone.

Maybe it was just his imagination.

He wasn't sure.

Barry pulled his blankets back up.

He set the Zoombla! action figure back on the nightstand.

But he left the green light on.

He tossed right and left.

The night was quiet.

Barry closed his eyes, just a little.

Skrt, skrt, skrt.

Barry opened his eyes again. He must have been sleeping.

Skrt, skrt, skrt.

This was for real. Something was scratching.

"Hello?" Barry whispered.

The noise stopped. He reached for the nightstand.

His Zoombla! action figure was gone.

He reached for the cord to the lamp.

His fingers touched something hairy, but the fur was slick and wet.

"Ewww!" Barry pulled his fingers back.

He stood up on the bed and shook his hand off.

What the heck did he touch?

Skrt, skrt, skrt.

Was it a mouse or a rat or something?

He reached higher this time, and found the dangling cord. He yanked it and yellow light flooded the room.

Barry looked on the nightstand. Nothing was there except the lamp. The Zoombla! action figure had fallen to the floor.

Barry reached his hand out to pick it up, but then he jerked his hand back.

What was that weird thing he touched?

He hopped down from the bed and looked underneath.

It looked like a little shadow moved, but it was too hard to tell.

Barry pulled the top off his lamp so that the bulb was sticking out of the metal rod, all alone.

He pushed it under the bed.

Nothing there.

The white fluffy part underneath the mattress started smoking. He pulled the lamp back and set it on the nightstand.

He tiptoed to the door and opened it.

Nothing outside.

Barry closed the door and put the shade back on the lamp. He crawled into bed and pulled the blankets up close.

He closed his eyes, but the light was too bright.

Barry opened his eyes and pulled the sheet off the bed. He threw the sheet over the lamp, so the light wasn't so bright.

Satisfied, he pulled the blankets up again and went to sleep.

Barry woke up drowsy when a little mosquito landed on his chin. He swatted at it, then tried to relax.

A few minutes later, he felt a little tickle on his cheek. He brushed it with his palm and shook his head.

A little sharp pain poked Barry in his gums. He put his hand up to his mouth and there was the same slick, wet furry thing.

Barry opened his eyes and adjusted to the dim light.

A little creature was standing on his chin, prying his lips open. Another little creature had both hands inside Barry's mouth!

One more of these things was standing on Barry's shoulder. It had both arms wrapped around a tooth!

Barry slapped his hand to his mouth.

The little creatures dodged and dove into the blankets.

Skrt, skrt, skrt!

Their little clawed toes scampered across the wood floor.

"BOB!" Barry screamed as loud as he could. He stood up on the bed and kicked the blankets.

Skrt, skrt skrt!

The little creatures disappeared under the cracks of the door.

"Bob! Heb be!" Barry shouted.

Barry poked at his mouth. It felt weird. Different.

He reached a finger inside. He poked at his bottom two front teeth. Then he ran his fingers around smooth soft tissue. He felt the top and the bottom of his gums.

Barry's mom opened the door. "Barry, what's going on? Did you call for mom, or Bob?" she laughed quietly and yawned.

"Heb be, peed. Peed heb. By peef a ow godd." Barry stood in the middle of his bed, shaking. "I hab mo peef."

"I don't understand, Bear Bear," said his mom. She walked to Barry and picked him up with a grunt, setting him in her lap. "Are you just playing a joke?"

She stroked his back.

Barry slowly opened his mouth.

All his teeth were gone, except for the bottom front two.

Barry's mom opened her eyes wide and gasped. "What happened, Little Bear?"

Barry relaxed and rested his head on his mom's shoulder. "I bom bo."A long string of drool flooded out.

From that angle he could see inside her mouth. It looked like she had two rows of teeth, with little child's teeth stuck behind her adult ones – except for the bottom front two.

9 – GATOR COUNTRY

Lurita sat back in her paddleboat, facing up at the sun. Her dark black face was covered in a nice Sunday hat, even though it was only Friday. It cast a broad shadow over her pretty pink dress.

A big, burly man paddled the boat. His face was covered in patches of mud from sleeping on the ground. Little branches and straw stuck out of his raggedy hair.

His meaty hand dropped an oar for the moment

Lurita lowered her chin and looked at the brute. "Boy, if you don't keep this vessel nice and straight, I'll see to it you get a whippin' you never forget."

The burly man nodded and wrenched the oar back into place with a loud squeak of grinding metal. "Don't mind no whippin'," he said. "You just keep you hex to youself."

Lurita lifted up her hand and spread her fingers, pointing the tips at the brute.

The burly man looked away and mumbled prayers under his breath.

Quiet as a mouse, a little boy sat with eyes glued open, watching everything. Back and forth, his head darted.

As they slowed he looked over the edge of the boat, pointing.

"It's gator country," said Lurita. "Better expect a few gators. And that one is hungry." She leaned in close to the boy. "Boo!"

The boy jumped with fright and almost toppled over the side and into the water.

"I'm just foolin', boy," said Lurita. "We gonna fix you up right. But you keep them arms in away from them gators, for real."

The paddleboat slowed to a stop, the nose rubbing

up against an old wooden dock, ravaged by time.

Lurita and the boy pulled up and out of the boat, dodging the missing planks as they walked across the warped ones. The wood creaked and groaned, like it was trying to tell them to keep out.

They made their way to a hut, falling apart at every joint. Some boards were slanted and others were missing altogether. It looked like the timber was trying to plant roots and become a tree again.

Outside, a dirty little girl sat on a chair with a broken back end. She cupped her face in her hands. She perked up when she saw the visitors. She held up one hand. "Witch busy."

Lurita smacked the girl's hand away. Electricity crackled when their skins touched. "Witch never busy. She a lazy one." She pushed her way through the ramshackle door and into the hut.

Inside was a disaster of a mess. Half-filled bottles and jars set on about any flat surface there was. Melted candle wax ran down the side of a stool and live animals crept and crawled every which way.

Mice and rats, centipedes and frogs all came alive at the step of the intruders. They paid no mind to humans, walking and hopping over them like they owned the place, and it looked like they did.

Disguised as a statue, a young woman sitting on a table swayed gently. Her eyes were closed. She opened them slow like and frowned when she saw Lurita. She reached up to her neck and grabbed onto a leather pouch.

The girl was pretty, but covered in mud. Her hair looked like it had never met a brush, and her fingernails were long and pointy. Her eyes burned like there was a fire inside, waiting to get out.

"Lurita," she said. "Why you come round here?" She held her neck pouch up

"Nice to see you too, Witch," said Lurita. "Brought you a customer."

The little boy reached into his pockets and pulled out a few jangly coins.

"Witch don't need money," she cackled. "Just need to borrow the boy's smile for a spell." She reached out and touched the little boy's face.

His smile sank into a question. "Is this voodoo?" he asked. His voice was high and chirpy, like a squirrel.

"No, boy," said the witch. "This hoodoo. This the good magic of the swamp heart." She pointed her finger at Lurita. "That the bad one that do voodoo. Witch tell her no voodoo."

She reached down and put her hand on the boy's shoulder. "Now how witch can help you?" she asked.

Lurita stepped down hard on a rat. Her nice shoes squished part of its tail. The rat squealed and flipped on its back, trying to defend itself but Lurita only stepped down harder.

"His mama done run off again," she said. "Told me he wants her back for good. I said I can help but he want to see you."

The witch nodded. "Maybe this boy see you magic and know you never help," she said. She reached back and grabbed a jar of eggs, sitting in a yellow liquid. She opened the top and it smelled like farts mixed with rotten swamp gas.

"Eat one them," the witch said. "Every night you wake up when the moon be high. You go to the graveyard where you grandmamma buried and you say out loud 'bring me mama keep. Bring me mama deep.' Then you mama come back and stay around."

The boy reached in and grabbed an egg. He lifted it to his mouth. His body shook and he dry barfed a little.

The witch nodded.

The boy put the egg in his mouth and tried to

swallow it whole. He couldn't. Coughing and gagging he chewed it and swallowed, retching a little afterward.

"That be all," said Lurita. She walked outside and the boy followed.

The dirty girl sat on the edge of the dock witch a bucket of stinky fish heads. She was picking up the fish heads and throwing them into the water.

A swarm of gators rolled lazily through the water, snapping and rolling over on one another trying to snatch up the fish heads.

"What you name, girl?" demanded Lurita.

"Lurita," said the girl. She didn't even look back at them.

Lurita steamed. "Don't you sass me, girl." She reached out and touched her shoulder. Sparks shot between the two and crackled in the damp air.

The dirty girl offered a fish head to the little boy.

The little boy held onto the fish head. He watched the girl launch another one out into the marsh. Then he picked his up and tossed it.

"I never see you around here," said Lurita. "No need to make another enemy. That's what I says. Now tell me, girl. What is your name?"

"The little girl stood up and turned around to face them. "My name Lurita," she said again.

Lurita stamped on the old dock and it creaked in agony. She reached into her little skin satchel and pulled out a necklace. It was made from snail shells and little pebbles with holes in the center. It was dark and basic, but pretty in its own way.

Lurita handed the necklace to the girl. "Let's make nice," she said. "You wear this and make yourself all pretty like."

The dirty little girl palmed the necklace and looked at it. She smiled and revealed a slew of missing teeth.

She looped the necklace over her sticking out every

which way hair, then pulled it down to rest on her shoulders.

Lurita laughed a cruel laugh.

The necklace shrank. The dirty girl looked at Lurita, begging for something. Her fingers shot up to the charm and she clutched at it.

The girl gasped and grabbed for the necklace, but it got tighter and tighter the more she struggled. It started to get so tight it closed off her air. She knocked over the chair and fell backwards onto the dock.

One of her legs kicked up and she tipped through a big gap in the dock, splashing into the water below.

The hungry alligators dipped their eyes under the water and disappeared.

The witch poked her head out of the hut. "Now what goin' on out here?" she cried. She looked down at the dirty girl, splashing in the water and reaching up for the dock. She couldn't quite get her fingers over the lip of the wood.

A big gator mouth lifted up out of the water and snapped shut on the girl.

Lurita shrugged her shoulders. "That the end of that girl," she said. "And she took my necklace."

"That girl is no girl," laughed the witch. "She a simulacrum."

"A what?"

The witch spit a gob of brown tobacco and saliva. "That girl be you. I made she from you hair. She supposed to help guard this abode from you and you black voodoo."

Lurita tried to breathe but the air wouldn't come to her. Her eyes opened wide. She put her hands to her throat.

The little boy looked between Lurita and the witch. His hands fumbled in his pockets, trying to wipe off the fish slime.

The witch laughed again. "Witch told you no voodoo. Now you done done no good."

The Headless Fox

5

SCARE-OMETER

10 – THE HEADLESS FOX

Brianna lay down in the leaves. Her arms and legs dangled over piles of red, purple and brown. She smiled and looked up at the pretty autumn colors.

Isaac lay down a few feet away from her. He smiled and looked over at Brianna.

She was very pretty for twelve years old.

In three years he would be as old as her.

When they were both twelve, then he could ask her out on a date.

Above them, a squirrel ran out onto the edge of a branch. It pointed its whiskered nose down at the two intruders.

Brianna waved to the squirrel. "Hi, friend!" she said pleasantly.

The squirrel chippered and cracked a walnut in its paws, tossing down bits of shell at them.

Isaac rolled over, dodging the well-aimed fragments. "Hey! I like you too, squirrel. Why you gotta throw stuff at me?"

He laughed and rolled onto his knees, standing up.

Brianna joined him. "Head rush!" she said.

"You want to come over for dinner?" asked Isaac. "My mom is making roast beef and potatoes."

"Not tonight," said Brianna. "My mom is working late, so she's going to order pizza."

"Not fair," said Isaac. "Can I come over for dinner?"

"Sure," said Brianna. "Sometimes mom doesn't even have time to sit down and eat with me. She sits at the table with her computer and works, works, works."

"Not my mom," said Isaac. "She just sits and watches TV all day. And then all night too. And she eats ice cream, and she doesn't even share."

Brianna picked up a stick and pointed it at Isaac. "Maybe your mom could teach my mom how to stop working and watch TV." She poked Isaac with the stick.

Isaac laughed and tried to push away the stick. He reached down and grabbed his own stick. "Maybe your mom could teach my mom to stop watching TV and do some work."

Brianna tapped her stick against Isaac's. The fight was on.

They rapped sticks, dodging around trees, thrusting and blocking.

Brianna knocked Isaac's stick out of his hand.

Isaac fell backwards into the leaves. He put his hands up, breathing heavily.

"Do you yield?" asked Brianna. She pointed her stick at his chest.

"Maybe," said Isaac. "What does yield mean?"

"It means give up," said Brianna.

"I don't ever give up!" Isaac grabbed the stick.

Brianna pushed the stick deeper until it dug into Isaac's stomach. Isaac tried to hold it, but the force knocked the wind out of him.

"I give up," Isaac said, sucking in air.

Brianna smiled and tossed the stick away. She reached down and helped Isaac up.

"Thanks," said Isaac. He put one leg behind Brianna's and pushed her into the leaves. "Sucker!" He laughed.

Brianna rolled over. "Oww!" she grabbed at her knee.

Isaac's heart skipped a beat. He kneeled down beside her. "Are you okay, Brianna? I'm so sorry I was just having fun." He put his hand on her knee.

Brianna whirled her hands around his and laid Isaac sprawling on his back. She rolled over on top of him. "Just kidding," she smiled. She held his hands in place. "Sucker."

Isaac blushed. He struggled to resist Brianna's grasp, but she was much bigger and stronger. "It's getting kind of dark," he said. "Maybe we should go back to your house."

Brianna let go. "We could," she said. "Or we could look for fireflies."

They both looked up as a firefly flashed, then disappeared against the trees of the same color. Their eyes rested on a fox, not far from them.

Brianna got off of Isaac and he rolled to his knees.

The fox was sitting on its haunches, staying perfectly still. Its red fur with white and black patches was well groomed. But the most glaring and strange thing about this fox, was that the head was missing.

"I didn't see that there when we got here," said Brianna.

"Maybe it's fake," said Isaac. He took a step forward and reached for the fox.

The fox took a step back and lowered its body to all fours. It dragged its front paws through the leaves.

Brianna and Isaac looked at each other.

"This is really happening, right?" asked Brianna. "Oww!"

Isaac pinched Brianna. "Just in case. Oww!"

Brianna pinched him back.

The fox kept walking backwards. It had a wound where the head had once been attached. The flesh had reconnected and a purple scar zagged out from the center.

Brianna and Isaac followed it slowly as it walked backward through the woods. Then, it turned around and walked forward. The back end was completely intact.

"That's pretty gross," whispered Isaac. "I thought a fox couldn't live without its head."

"It might not be alive," whispered Brianna.

"Why are we following it?" whispered Isaac.

"Why are we whispering?" whispered Brianna. "It doesn't have ears."

Isaac laughed. "You're right," he said. "Maybe it needs help."

"Yeah, help finding its head," said Brianna. "He doesn't have eyes."

The fox darted through the woods, dodging rocks and trees.

Brianna ran faster. She was a few yards behind the fox.

"But it seems like it can see," Isaac called. He struggled to keep up.

The woods grew darker.

"Maybe we shouldn't follow this thing," said Isaac. He was breathing hard.

The fox stopped at the edge of a hill.

Outside a small cave, the fox turned to face them again. It pawed at the leaves. Then it went back to sitting on its haunches. It seemed like it was waiting for them.

Brianna shrugged. "Maybe it lost its head in this cave."

"Too weird," said Isaac. "I'm kind of scared. And it's getting really dark."

"Are you scared of the dark?" asked Brianna. "We're pretty close to home."

Isaac shook his head. "I'm not scared of the dark. I'm scared of this fox that's missing its head. That's really creepy. And why does it need our help? It seems like it can run around the forest just fine."

Brianna lay down on the leaves outside the cave. "Yeah but this is fun!" she said. "What an adventure. I wish we had a camera."

Isaac lay down next to her. "I wish we had a flashlight."

"Yeah," said Brianna. "It's really dark in here." She put her hand inside the cave. It was warm and wet. She yanked her hand out. "Eww!"

"What?" asked Isaac. "Now you're scared?"

"Gross, touch it!" said Brianna.

Isaac put his hand in the cave. "Why is it warm in here?"

"I don't know," said Brianna. "I can't see anything."

Fireflies flicked on and off around them. One flashed inside the cave.

"Whoa," said Isaac. "This cave is small, but super deep."

He stuck his head inside the cave.

"Really?" Brianna stuck her head inside the cave, too.

CHOMP!

The cave bit down.

Isaac and Brianna didn't even have time to scream.

Isaac and Brianna lay still in the leaves with their heads off. Their bodies kicked and jerked with a spasm here and there.

Two yellow eyes flickered open on the hillside.

The cave swallowed their heads.

The headless fox walked forward and pawed dry leaves over Brianna, then Isaac.

11 – ALL GONE

Brady sat in a fold up chair outside his blue tent. He held his dad's phone, playing video games.

Brady's dad bent down on his hands and knees. He leaned and blew into the fire pit.

Ash flew up into his face, but smoke came with it. With a few more puffs, a tiny fire jumped out and lit the kindling.

Brady set his foot out and pushed it into his dad's butt.

Brady's dad fell forward into the tiny fire and put it out. His face was covered in black soot.

"Oops," said Brady. "Sorry, dad. I didn't see you there." He smiled.

Brady's dad smeared char across his face, trying to rub it off. "Be more careful, please Brady. That's not the first time you've knocked us over this weekend. Maybe you're growing faster than you think."

Brady ignored his dad, crunching a handful of cheesy popcorn.

"Brady," said his dad. "You're not using up all my phone battery, are you?"

Brady looked at the phone. It only had 5% battery power left. It was flashing red. "Nope," he said. "Plenty of juice."

Brady's sister tried to squeeze between the fire pit and his fold up chair.

Brady put his foot out at the last moment and it caught between his sister's legs.

She fell down and skinned her knee.

"You nincompoop!" she yelled. "Didn't you listen to what dad just told you?"

"Yeah," replied Brady. "He told me to be careful.

Maybe you should listen to him you big clumsy ogre."

Brady's sister stamped her foot. "I am not clumsy, meanie!" She reached over to punch Brady but he leaned the chair over. Her fist went too far and she tripped over the chair, falling in his lap.

"Clumsy, clumsy," said Brady. He pushed her off of him. "You should be more careful." Brady chuckled.

Brady's sister landed on her skinned knee and held both hands over it, trying to stop the blood.

"BRADY!" his mom yelled.

"WHAT?" he yelled back.

"Get over here and help me clean this fish," she waved a fillet knife in the air. "And stop calling your sister ugly."

"I didn't call her ugly this time," Brady said. "I called her clumsy." He stepped over his sister. "But you are ugly," he whispered to his sister.

"And you're stupid," she shot back.

Brady walked out to the dock.

His mom sat next to a pile of fish guts. She was cutting into the last fish. "Would you please bring these fillets to your dad so he can grill them?"

"Mom," said Brady. "Why do I have to do everything around here?"

His mom waved the fillet knife toward him. "And when you're done," she added, "come get these fish entrails and throw them way out into the water so the fish can eat them."

Brady laughed. "Why do you have to call guts entrails?"

His mom sighed and looked up at him. "If you don't throw the entrails into the water, raccoons and bears and who knows what are going to smell them and come to our campsite and keep looking for food. You know what I'm saying?"

Brady humphed and brought the fillets to his dad.

He washed his hands.

Brady's mom walked up with the last of the fillets. She sidled up next to Brady and washed her hands, looking at him.

"I know, I know!" said Brady. He walked back out to the end of the dock.

Flies were buzzing around the bloody mess his mom left. There were bones, twisted purple strings and little fish organs, still fresh and sticky.

"Dinner's ready!" his dad called to him.

Brady sniffed his nose and turned his back on the icky pile. He left the guts sitting in a squishy heap.

Brady's family sat eating fish sandwiches and barbecue chips. His sister stood up from the table when he got there and dodged him.

Brady sat down and looked at his plate of food. He pushed it a few inches away.

Everyone looked at Brady, eating in quiet.

"This camping trip sucks," said Brady. "I wish it were just me." He pushed his plate even further away from him.

Brady's dad finished the last of his sandwich and licked his fingers. He talked around a big bite he was chewing. "You would be bored out of your mind if you were all alone."

"No way," said Brady. "I wish you were all gone." He pushed the plate one more time and it slipped off the edge of the table. The fish landed in the dusty dirt. The chips pattered down around it.

"Rude," said his mom. "Clean it." She stood up and cleared her place at the table.

"I'll clean it in the morning," said Brady. "It's pretty much already dark."

The sun dipped behind the pine trees, turning orange before it disappeared.

"Well then, I guess you two can go to sleep early,"

said Brady's mom.

"I'm sleeping with mom and dad tonight," said Brady's sister.

Brady's dad looked at his mom. She shrugged her shoulders.

They all went to sleep.

Brady went to his tent alone.

He stayed awake reading scary stories.

He pulled out his dad's phone from his pocket.

He put on headphones and listened to music.

Headlights flashed through the tent.

A car thrummed and rumbled away.

Brady pulled the headphones out of his ears.

Silence.

Not even the birds chirped at night, way up here.

Brady didn't remember anyone else at the campsite.

He unzipped his tent and peeked his head outside.

It was very dark. The clouds covered up the moon and the stars.

Brady took out his dad's phone and flicked the flashlight on.

The light revealed an empty campsite.

Everything was packed up.

His parents' tent was gone.

The car was gone.

Only the flattened dirt where his dad shoveled it remained.

Brady looked around the campgrounds.

Nobody else was here.

The flashlight went out.

A little red flashing battery icon appeared on the screen.

The phone died.

And then there was darkness.

Total darkness.

Brady put his hands out in front of his face. He could not see them.

He stepped outside the tent, tripping on the bottom edge of the zipper.

He could not see the ground in front of him.

In the distance, something thumped.

It was like wood on wood, thumping, thumping, but it was going away.

Then squelching. Liquids and solids getting slurped up.

The guts! Something was eating the guts!

The squelching stopped.

Brady remembered his fish sandwich. Whatever that thing was would surely come for the sandwich next.

Brady staggered around the campsite, his bare feet stepping on little stones and sharp pinecones.

He kicked something solid and stubbed his toe.

"Oww," he cried. He covered his mouth, then reached down to pick up the fish sandwich.

His hand went into the fire pit, his fingers sliding across hot coals buried under the cool ash.

"OWW!" he cried louder.

Oh no.

He put both hands over his mouth. His right hand was stinging with pain.

The thumping, thumping, started again.

The thing must still be hungry.

It was getting closer.

Then the thumping stopped.

It must be off the dock.

Crackle, crackle, little stones under the heavy foot of something big.

Something getting closer.

What the heck am I doing here? **Brady thought.**

I should go inside the tent and zip it up!

No, that's a terrible idea.

I should run!

Except Brady couldn't see anything.

He stayed still.

This was a bad idea.

Heavy breathing.

Maybe it was a bear.

A strange smell filled the air. Like old milk and dirty laundry.

Dank. His mom would say dank. She was always using stupid words. Big words.

His mom was stupid. So was his dad. And his sister.

How could they leave him here like this?

The thing stopped breathing for a moment, sniffing. It brushed its huge body against the creaking picnic table.

It gobbled the fish sandwich, slurping, munching, chewing.

Then the quiet returned.

What the heck was it doing?

Brady realized he still had both hands over his mouth.

He let go.

He was shaking now.

This thing must be as big as three people.

It must still be hungry.

Brady launched forward, running as fast as his feet would carry him.

He ran blind, through the dark, ripping past bushes and into the forest.

Over the stones he ran, his feet past the point of pain.

No time to see if that thing was still behind him.

Brady ran faster and faster, until he thwacked his head into a tree.

Yellow stars appeared. His neck hurt.

Something warm was dripping down his forehead and into his eyes.

He had to keep going.

Brady felt dizzy.

He couldn't run any more.

He had to crawl on all fours. His burnt hand plodded along, leading the way for his scratched up feet and legs.

And then the cold, wet lake lapped his forearms.

He was at the lake!

Maybe this thing couldn't swim.

Brady grit his teeth. It was hard to think.

It was time to go to sleep.

Brady pushed forward into the water. He swam about four strokes.

His eyes drooped.

Too many stars.

His head hurt.

It was time to go to sleep.

Brady sank down into the lake and went to sleep.

At the campsite, Brady's dad turned on a lantern.

His mom looked inside his tent.

His sister held his mom's hand.

"Brady?" called his dad. "Just kidding! You said you wanted to be all alone, but we would never leave you out here in the middle of nowhere."

House of Bones

6
SCARE-OMETER

12 – HOUSE OF BONES

When the bell rang, Tucker couldn't wait to stand up and run for the door. His backpack was already on. He had been staring out the window for an hour.

"Wait! The homework..." Mrs. Krantz called after him.

Too late. She had her chance.

He let the door swing behind him and ran through the halls.

Tucker was the first one out. Usually the hall had shoving room only at the end of a long school week.

He jumped down the five steps leading to the doors outside.

The lazy crossing guards were just now getting out of their chairs and stretching.

Tucker ran across the driveway where a long line of cars was backed up, bumper to bumper.

He squeezed between two minivans and made off across the grass to the two-foot chain link fence. It was only there to tell you when you were leaving school property.

Tucker hopped the fence and his backpack landed with a thump on his butt. He liked wearing the straps low because the cushioning had come off when he threw it off a rooftop when he was climbing down.

Today was a special day.

Some really mean kids had been teasing the handicapped ones, the really nice kids in special ed. It had nothing to do with Tucker, except that he couldn't watch it happen.

He wanted to stand up for the handicapped kids, but he knew if he did, the mean kids would all turn on him. They would make his life miserable.

He had seen it happen a few times before.

The whole school had seen it. That's why nobody tried to play the hero.

But it still broke Tucker's heart listening to heckling and watching them play mean pranks and laughing at defenseless kids. Nice kids who were born different.

So he had taken to sneaking off school grounds for lunch.

So had this girl.

Her name was Lilith. He had never seen her at school. But they had to rotate subjects in seventh grade because the school was short on money. So that wasn't too crazy.

But she was really nice. Really white. Super pale. Long black hair.

She said she came from the North. She had an accent, so it was hard to tell. Mostly she just listened.

And Tucker loved talking, so it was perfect. He told her stories about when he was a little boy, where to eat in town if she didn't know yet, how not to get teased in school.

He told her he wanted to help those handicapped kids and she said she might know how. Of course, she didn't say how, so maybe she didn't understand him. Maybe she didn't understand anything he said.

But she was pretty. And she was a girl.

And she told Tucker to come meet her in the woods on Friday after school.

She said she wanted to give him a kiss.

Maybe. Unless her accent made is sound like that. But why else would a girl invite you to come into the woods alone with her?

She said to come alone.

Tucker was alone.

He saw her sitting on a fallen log. Her dress was so

neatly ironed. It was black. She loved black. Unless she didn't love black and her parents just bought her a bunch of black clothes without asking her and then she had to wear it because she didn't have anything else.

'You're thinking too much, Tucker,' **thought Tucker.**

Lilith stood up.

"Hi, Lilith!" said Tucker. He put his hands in his pockets.

She nodded her head.

How did she beat Tucker from school? Unless she skipped her last class.

Maybe she was one of those bad kids! Tucker's mom had said to stay away from those bad kids. But she was pretty.

Tucker should make an exception for a pretty, bad kid. Especially one that might have asked him to come to the woods alone so she could give him a kiss.

Lilith turned her back and walked away from Tucker.

Tucker followed. "So, did you want to give me a kiss?"

"Keess," said Lilith, without even turning back to face him.

She was a weird one. But hey, aren't we all?

Tucker followed her quietly walking through the woods. His sneakers crunched through the leaves. Winter was coming.

Lilith walked silently, almost like her feet were floating.

Tucker tried to catch up so he could catch her eye. It was hard to walk with his hands in his pockets. But it made it easy for him to clamp his armpits together. He was sweating, but it felt cold. "Did you want to, right here? Or somewhere special?"

"Spesha," said Lilith. She didn't even look over to see him.

"It's my first kiss," said Tucker. "So anywhere we kiss is going to be special for me."

Lilith stopped walking. She turned to face Tucker. She was hard to read. She never smiled.

"Keess," she said.

"Yeah, totally!" Tucker closed his eyes. He puckered up.

His heart was beating out of control.

He could feel the armpit sweat going down past his waist and into his underwear.

He leaned forward.

He waited.

Nothing happened.

He opened his eyes.

Lilith was holding up a small ring of keys right in front of his face. They were all white and it looked like they weren't made of metal. The ring was made of some braided red rope. "Keess," she repeated.

"Oh," Tucker blushed. He brought his face back over his shoulders. "Keys. Right. Got it." He reached up and grabbed the key ring.

The forest floor shook.

Tucker held onto the keys. His knees quaked. He tried to stay upright.

He reached for Lilith's hand.

She stood still, calmly observing.

Her hand was cold.

In front of them, bones erupted from the ground.

Hundreds.

Thousands.

Human bones. Skulls, arms, legs, spines, everything you could imagine. Animal bones were mixed in, along with horns and tusks and about any kind you could imagine.

Tucker realized he wasn't breathing. He was squeezing Lilith's hand, hard. He took a deep breath.

"Home," Lilith turned to face him.

"That's?" Tucker tried to ask. It wasn't a full question. He let go of her hand. She was so calm. "This is your home?"

He looked down at the keys in his hand. White, hard, smooth. They were probably also made of bone.

Lilith walked up onto the front step. Broad and jagged, bones protruded this way and that. She approached the wide double doors at the front.

"Why am I holding the key?" Tucker asked. This was the scariest moment of his life so far. And maybe the most disappointing. Instead of getting a kiss, he ended up outside some nightmare bone castle with the girl he liked standing at the front door.

Lilith stood next to the doors. "Chooss," she said.

Tucker walked up toward the step. The closer he got, the more detail he could see. Little squirrel bones and bird wing bones filled in the gaps where the larger bones settled. "Choose what?" he asked.

"Open," said Lilith. "Don't open." She placed her hand on the door. Her hands were the color of bone. Standing so close to the house was like camouflage.

Maybe that's why she was so white. Maybe she wasn't even alive. But there she was, breathing and looking at him. She seemed as alive as any other girl at his school.

Tucker felt the keys in his hand. Now his hands were sweating. The keys were cold no matter how long he held onto them. "What happens if I open the door?" he asked. "It's not much of a choice if I don't know what happens, right?"

He didn't dare step up and join her. It was too scary. And who knows what was behind those doors?

"You," Lilith said. "Open. You get strong. Get magic."

"Oh," said Tucker. "And if I don't open?"

"No magic," replied Lilith.

That one seemed obvious.

He willed himself to lift up one leg and step foot on the bone step. His foot instantly tingled with pins and needles prickling inside. He hopped up. Same thing with the other foot.

"So I get the magic for free?" asked Tucker. "Or does something bad happen? Because it seems like something really bad would happen if I opened this door."

"No bad," said Lilith. "You be magic. You be like me." She put her hand on his heart. "Ba bop. Ba bop. Poof!" she gestured an explosion with her hands.

Tucker's heart slowed. He put his hand on Lilith's heart. There was no beat. His hand was also close to her boob. It was the closest it had ever been to a boob. His heart started going faster. He pulled his hand away.

"So if I open the door, I die?" he asked. "But I get magic powers because I'm kind of alive, like you."

Lilith nodded her head. "And people not see you like how alive," she added. "Goodbye, family."

Tucker nodded. "My family wouldn't understand and they would be freaked out and then who knows what, right? The town might burn down our house or they might all kill me. I think I understand. Do you have magic?"

Electricity sparked off Lilith's shoulders and travelled down her arms, arcing between her hands. She rose up off the ground. Her eyes turned a deep purple color and wings sprouted from her back. They unfolded and shadowed deep darkness over the bone.

She opened her mouth and Tucker saw rows of sharp teeth and a forked snake tongue. This was pretty cool stuff.

"Get magic, but no family." Puffs of smoke came out Lilith's nose. She was a really pretty demon, too.

"Want Tucker family."

Tucker thought about it. He watched her. He wanted to be like her. But he would have to give up his family. They wouldn't want a demon for a son. Would they?

No.

But he could get revenge on all those bullies.

With powers like that, he could get revenge on all the bullies, everywhere!

Of course, Lilith had asked him to come into the woods for a simple kiss. What would happen if he opened the door and went inside this freak fest? Was Lilith just going to eat him when he got in there? Or worse?

Tucker lifted the key and walked toward the double doors. As the key came near, the little animal skull that was a knob opened its mouth.

Tucker put the key into the skull's mouth and twisted the lock.

Far Out

7

SCARE-OMETER

13 – FAR OUT

"Wear your life jacket, sweetie." Abby's mom reached out to fasten the buckles.

"Leave me alone, mom!" Abby pulled away.

Abby's mom crossed her arms. "You're not wearing it for me, you're wearing it for you. If you fall in the water..."

"I know how to swim, mom," Abby walked down the dock toward the boat. "I'm thirteen years old. God damn it."

Abby's mom dropped her jaw. "You do not talk to your mother like that, missy. You are not going on that boat."

Abby laughed and ran to the end of the dock. She hopped into the little motorboat.

Abby's mom ran after her.

Abby took off her life jacket and threw it at her mom. It landed in the water.

The boys in the boat revved the engine and the motorboat sped off across the calm, cool water.

"You are in so much trouble!" her mom called after her.

The sun shined hot rays down on everyone. The short teenager at the front took off his shirt. The wind whipped the shirt out of his hand and it flew back into the lake. He reached back to try to grab it. He had little yellow peach fuzz growing on his chest.

"No turning back now!" called Blake. He was driving the boat as fast as it could go. His sunglasses started to lift up off his nose, so he tilted his head down.

Abby smiled and raised both hands up. She scooted back in her seat so the wind wouldn't life her out of the boat, too.

The lake was enormous. Clear, flat, blue-green water surrounded by Alpine air and tall mountains. Dark green pine trees circled the bay, then disappeared in the distance as they sped out toward the center.

"I've never seen a lake this big!" yelled Abby over the thrum of the engine.

Blake reached into his pocket and held out a compass. "Good thing I brought this!" he yelled back. "Once you're in the middle, you can't see the shore."

The wind picked up the compass and it pinged onto the motor, bouncing backwards to plop into the lake.

Blake let go of the handle. The motorboat lost speed instantly.

The short boy up front launched backward and hit his head on the wooden seat in the middle as he toppled to the deck. "Oww!" he shouted. "Who taught you to drive?"

"Oh no," said Abby. She regained her balance and looked over the side.

Blake stood up on the back edge of the boat, watching the compass sink. "Oh well," he said. "We can use the sun to figure out where we are." He put one hand back on the handle and pulled the cord for the motor.

The motor idled for a moment, then sputtered out.

The short boy rubbed his head. "What?" he looked at Blake.

Blake shook his head. He looked up. Grey clouds were washing over the sky and blocking the sun.

"What?" repeated the short boy. "I didn't fill the tank, but you didn't ask me to. It's your stupid boat anyways."

"That's your only job," said Blake. "Alright, whatever. We might not have much time for this." He reached down and took out a wake board and rope.

"Ladies first?" He handed it to Abby.

Abby blushed. "I'm not very good."

Blake pushed harder.

Abby took the board. The boat wobbled as she leaned over the side and dipped her legs into the water. "Ooh!" She dove in, leaning over the wakeboard as she surfaced. "This water is really brisk."

"I think it just melted off the mountains," said Blake. He tossed Abby the rope and she grabbed the handle at the end.

"Okay," said Blake. "I'll start out slow, then pick up speed when it seems like you've got it. Just wave when you want me to turn around and get you."

"Got it," said Abby. She tensed up, holding the handle tight. She dug her knees into the board.

Blake pulled the cord again and revved the engine. It purred softly. He twisted the handle slightly and the boat pulled forward slowly.

When the rope was taught, the wakeboard rode up to the top and skimmed across the water. Abby followed the boat, sending ripples on either side of the wake board.

Blake turned the handle and gave the boat some speed.

Abby held on tight as the boat turned, sending rippling waves coming right for her. She thumped up over the waves and landed with a splash back on the surface.

Abby leaned in and cruised across the flat middle to the wake on the other side. She rode up the side of the wake and surfed down the back of it.

"Yeah!" yelled Blake.

"I thought you said you weren't good!" shouted the short boy. He stood at the back of the boat, leaning on Blake's shoulder.

Abby laughed and looked up at them.

A huge gust of wind blew the boat so it tipped to the side. Blake and the short boy bunkered down into the boat, trying to steady it.

"Oww!" the short boy thumped his head into the side of the boat and his arm came over it, dragging in the water.

"Move!" Blake shouted. "You're so useless!"

Abby held on tight, trying to lean into the wind.

The nose of the board dug into the wake and Abby tipped up into the air for a moment, the board lost in the lake behind her. She closed her eyes and hit the water hard, plummeting down under.

Abby could hear the roar of the motorboat speed away from her, then grow faint in the distance.

She broke the surface with her head and gulped in air.

Pulling her hair back and wiping water from her eyes, Abby looked around.

The motorboat was gone.

She tread water and turned around in a full circle.

She couldn't see land.

The wind rippled the water, stinging her ears.

Not far behind her, the wakeboard bobbed up and down on the waves the boat had left behind.

Abby swam for the board. With each stroke, the wind seemed to blow it a bit further away.

Abby swam and swam. She stroked as hard as she could, trying to catch up.

Panting, she floated for a moment. Her breath came in hard against the chilly water.

The wakeboard was even further away than when she started. The wind blew it gently into the distance.

Abby raised up her arms and waved them in the air. "Blake!" she yelled. "I'm back here! Come get me please."

She laughed. Maybe they ran out of gas after all.

It wasn't that funny.

They would have to row back to where she was. But how would they know where to go without the compass?

Abby was a good swimmer. Maybe she could float back to shore, just kicking a little bit?

They would come back for her, even if they had to row. Blake was really strong.

Abby jerked her legs up.

Something slimy touched her foot. Like the top of a giant fish or a whale or something.

Abby took a deep breath in, floating as she paddled in circles.

Don't panic.

There aren't whales in this lake. But there are big fish. An drunk old fisherman told her he had caught a catfish that was twelve feet long.

But they don't eat people, do they?

She looked down into the clear blue water. Too hard to tell.

Abby breathed in and popped below the surface.

The cold water stung her eyes as she opened them. It was pretty clear for about an arms length but then it got really murky.

The familiar hum of the motorboat cruised in the distance.

They were here!

Abby surfaced and spit water out. She was getting tired.

"Blake. Blake! BLAKE!" Abby screamed the last one. "I'm over here! Come get me please!" She waved her hands frantically pedaling her feet to stay above water.

It was really cold in the lake.

She couldn't hear the motorboat above the surface. She couldn't see it either.

Abby looked around.

No shore.

No motorboat.

She dipped her ears underwater. The motorboat was close. But not that close.

Something brushed her foot again.

Abby jerked her legs back up. She was shaking. Maybe because it was so damn cold in the water. And the wind was frost burning her wet eyebrows.

Something kept brushing against her feet.

Something big.

Something soft. And scratchy. And wavy. And hungry.

Abby kicked hard, breaking the calm water.

She swam with the wind fast and far.

Looking past her thrashing feet, she couldn't see anything moving.

Maybe it was gone.

She stopped to catch her breath.

Her mom was right. She should have brought the damn life jacket.

Abby was so tired she couldn't paddle anymore. Just kick and float.

Maybe the monster was waiting for her to tire herself out.

Then it would eat her.

She was going to die out here!

Abby ducked her head underwater.

No monster.

She kicked at the surface, splashing down deeper into the darkness.

Her hands drifted across broad leafy seaweed. The thick slippery leaves swayed with her movement.

There was no monster. She had tired herself out swimming away from seaweed.

And the motor sound was back. It was getting closer!

Abby used the reserves of her strength to paddle up to the top.

She stopped a few inches before she got there.

Pushing, pushing she paddled hard but she was stuck.

Her ankle was caught in the seaweed.

Abby pulled her ankle as hard as she could, but it only jerked her body back down.

Above, the motorboat grew louder and louder. The shadow of the boats' hull came into view, speeding past Abby.

She looked up at the boat, snatching at the green rope wrapped around her.

Her last few bubbles drifted up. She watched them pop at the surface.

The boat motored on, into the darkness.

Crash

SCARE-OMETER

8

14 – CRASH

Jay held on to the guardrails and jumped. The bridge shook under his weight.

His family bounced up and down, grabbing the sides as they pushed their feet into the wooden boards.

"Stop," said his sister.

"What?" asked Jay. "It's fun!" He jumped again. The bridge shook.

His family held on tighter.

"Stop!" his sister yelled.

"What are you afraid of?" Jay asked. "Hundreds of people cross this bridge every day. Plenty of them are a lot fatter than you. Hard to believe." He jumped again.

"STOP!" yelled Jay's dad. "Your sister asked you already. There is no need to tease her and there is no need to keep shaking this bridge."

Jay jumped even higher. "Come back and make me."

"How am I related to you?" his sister asked. "You're such a jerk!"

"Why are you being mean to me?" Jay asked. His face was red and flustered. "I just want to shake things up because I think it's fun. And suddenly you guys all get to have it your way? Forget that! When do we ever get to have fun? This bridge is perfectly safe. They wouldn't have a bouncy bridge over a river in some canyon in the middle of nowhere if it wasn't safe to go on."

He jumped again.

His mom slipped and cut her knee on the wire. "You've been warned, Jake," she said. "You're grounded." She ran her hand along the side of her calf, catching the blood.

"Not until we get to the other side I'm not!" Jake laughed. He jumped up really high and hit the bridge hard.

His dad helped his mom up and took her hand all the way across, moving slowly.

His sister followed them, hand after hand.

Jake stayed in place. He jumped and jumped and jumped. He watched his family get smaller and smaller as they were closer to the other side. It was a ways. They bounced up and down like fleas as he jumped and landed and jumped and landed.

He was cracking himself up.

His family stood on the other side of the canyon.

"Jay," his mom called. "What are you waiting for?"

"I'm not coming!" he called back. "Are you crazy? You're just going to ground me."

His sister raised her arms up over her head. "What are you going to do, genius? Jump on the bridge forever? We're sick of waiting for you. Why don't you grow up already."

Jay jumped as high as he could. He brought his heels above the railing. His arms were supporting him now. But his heels were too high. He started to do a front summersault in the air except his left shoulder gave out.

Jay fell sideways, his neck smacking into the guardrail. He tried to grab the wires but he was confused and upside down.

He slipped over the side of the bridge, his body righting itself back up.

Now the weight of his legs were dragging him down over the side. He fell for a split second then caught the bottom of the bridge with one hand. It splintered and cut into his hand, he could feel it stinging.

"JAY!" his mother screamed in a shrill tone he had never heard before.

"Two hands, Jay!" his father yelled over her.

Jay reached up and grabbed the bridge with his other hand.

He looked down. It was hundreds of feet to the rocky, winding river beneath. This would be a fitting end. The bridge didn't break, it would be his own stupid fault for jumping so high.

His sister ran back onto the bridge, toward him.

With every step, the bridge bounced.

With every bounce, Jay's hands slipped a little.

He gripped hard with one hand, trying to lift the other hand higher up on the wooden ridge he was grasping.

"No!" Jay called. "You're too fat!"

When his sister got to the middle of the bridge, it creaked and groaned. It hadn't done that on the way over. She instinctively grabbed ahold of the metal wires.

PING! One wire snapped.

A chain reaction of PING! PING! PING! And wires snapped left and right. The bridge came apart directly in the center, flinging Jay to one side and his sister to the other.

They both lost their handholds and plummeted down, down, down.

The last sound they heard was their parents screaming as loud as they could, leaning over the edge of the canyon.

The Foundling

8

SCARE-OMETER

15 – THE FOUNDLING

Lila tugged on her dad's coat. He stood there talking to the shopkeeper.

She licked her ice cream and turned back down the alleyway, peering past the brick wall.

A little girl was digging garbage out of the trashcan behind the store. She sat in a puddle of her own pee.

"Dad," called Lila. "Seriously, you need to see this."

Lila's dad and the shopkeeper looked down the alley.

"Just leave that thing alone," said the shopkeeper. "They always come steal my rubbish."

"That's not a thing, it's a girl," said Lila's dad.

"Can we keep her?" asked Lila.

"No," said the shopkeeper. "The Cleaners come and put those things away. You just leave it. They bite you."

Lila's dad turned to face him. "Where would they put her?"

The shopkeeper crossed his arms. "That is dangerous thing! Cleaners put them away."

The little girl looked up at them. Underneath all the dirt and raggedy hair, she had very pretty brown eyes. She looked up at them, leaning behind the dumpster to hide.

Lila's dad put both hands on his head. "I'm going to regret this."

"Thank you daddy!" Lila hugged her dad, knocking the air out of him.

The shopkeeper shook his head and walked back

into his store.

The matter was settled. The foundling returned with them to their hotel room. Lila dropped pieces of her leftover lunch every few minutes. The girl scampered up to eat, then ran away from them again.

When they got to the room, the girl had warmed up a bit. Lila brought her inside and showed her how to shower. It took seven times before most of the grime came out of her hair and ears. Even afterwards it took a few weeks before the smell was completely gone.

*

Over the next six months, Lila trained the foundling while her dad was at work.

She showed her how to speak.

She put her own clothes on the raggedy girl.

She worked out with her to get some muscle back in her arms.

They ate every meal together.

They sang together.

They played together.

They did everything together.

The foundling would mimic everything Lila did with incredible accuracy.

One day, Lila's dad came home from work and found the two girls sitting side by side, wearing identical clothing.

"Hi dad! Look what I taught my new sister to do."

Lila's dad sat there looking at the two girls. "What am I watching?" he asked.

Lila stood up and pointed to the foundling. "That was her, daddy! Didn't she sound just like me?"

Lila's dad laughed. "Yeah, ha ha. Kind of scary. I couldn't even tell my own daughter apart from the... girl we found."

"My sister," said Lila.

"Sure," said Lila's dad. "In a manner of speaking, she is your sister." He got up and hugged Lila. "I'm really proud of you, baby. You have taken such good care of this girl. I mean, when we saw her there, nobody wanted her and she was a mess and now…"

He looked at the girl. "Now she looks and acts and talks just like you do. I'm really impressed."

"Thank you, daddy," said Lila. "That leads me to my next question. Can we take her home with us? I know we're leaving next week, but what's going to happen if we just go? Is she going to have to dig garbage out of the cans?"

"Whoa," said Lila's dad. "That's a lot of questions. I don't think she has to go back to the trashcans but you're asking to take home a human being. There are all kinds of legal issues like adoption and paperwork and a visa so she can become a citizen." He sat down and looked at both girls. "I'm not trying to use fancy adult words to confuse you. It is really complicated and we're not allowed to just take her, or any other person."

Lila's face drooped. "I thought you would say no."

Lila's dad smiled. "I want to honor your request but I don't think it's possible. Come get a hug sweetie. We can keep in touch and leave her with some nice things."

Lila leaned in and hugged her dad. "If she's not coming with, then I'm not going."

Lila's dad squeezed extra tight. "I respect that you're feeling so strongly about this and I want you to know that I am happy to help. But we can't take her with because it's like kidnapping and I could go to jail and she could be deported. It's not like a puppy."

*

A week later, the day had come for them to move

back home.

Lila's dad got back from work with a box of papers. "Hey, sweetie!" he called. He set the box down and walked into the kitchen.

Lila was washing blood off of her hands in the kitchen sink. "Hi father," she said. "I'm just making some dinner before we go to our home." She wiped more blood off the counter. Then she picked up a pan of meat and put it into the oven.

"Where's your new sister?" asked Lila's dad.

"I don't know," said Lila. "She ran off a few hours ago. But you're right. We shouldn't take her with. I like it when it's just me and you." She walked to her dad and hugged him.

"Oh," said Lila's dad. "A week ago you were pretty gung ho about taking her with."

"Yes, father," said Lila. She looked up into her dad's eyes. "But now I want you all to myself. And that dirty little rotten girl got what she deserves for wanting to leave me here all alone."

16 – COLD SHOULDER

It was a new moon, and the fall frost had settled on the grass already. Winter would be here soon.

The air smelled fresh and stung your nostrils. Dried leaves raked into piles rustled in the breeze.

Emma and Ava speed walked down the street.

Emma wore a thick jacket. She rubbed her hands together and blew into them. "Aren't you cold now?" she asked.

Ava wore a tank top with spaghetti straps. "Nope," she replied. "Maybe you're shaking because you're scared." Ava smiled.

"Scared of what?" Emma laughed. She looked around. Her teeth chattered.

"Scared of the dark," said Ava. "Mwa ha ha ha."

"Stop it, Ava," said Emma. "It is pretty scary out here."

"I'm not scared," said Ava. She slowed down.

"Come on!" Emma reached back and pulled Ava's arm. "My mom has hot cider waiting for us. And it's REALLY cold out."

A thick mist rolled in, through the trees, closing fast.

"Are you kidding me?" Emma shouted. "How could it get more cold and scary?"

"You could be getting eaten by zombies right now," Ava bit Emma's hand.

Emma screamed and it rang out in the night, echoing off the neighborhood houses. "So not funny!" she punched through the incoming mist, but whiffed through the air. "I just want to go home."

"Okay," said Ava. "Let's take the short cut. Through the graveyard."

They stood still.

Emma sniffled. "Not even you're brave enough to go through the graveyard."

"Oh yeah?"

"Yeah."

"I'll go through the graveyard," said Ava. "I'll even go first. But you have to come too."

"Nope," said Emma. "No way. Too scary. I'm already scared just thinking about it."

"I'll hold your hand," said Ava. "And I'll tell everyone at school that we did it and that you came and you weren't scared. And all the boys will think you're really brave and want to be your boyfriend."

"Eww," said Emma.

"All the boys except Tyler," said Ava. "Eww."

"Yeah," agreed Emma. "Eww. Well, maybe if he were nicer to girls. And if he didn't smell so bad. And if he wasn't always wearing ripped jeans."

"OOOH!" said Ava. "Someone LIKES Tyler!"

"No way," said Emma. "You mean, Tyler? Eww."

Ava walked up the street.

"That's not the way," said Emma.

"Yes it is," said Ava. She kept walking.

Emma followed her. "You're not serious right now, are you?"

Ava kept walking.

"There are dead people buried in there. Actual dead people!"

Ava kept walking.

Emma hustled to keep up. "And how are you going to see anything? You're probably going to trip over a gravestone. Even if nothing..."

Ava stopped. "If nothing what?" she asked.

"You know," said Emma. "Scary stuff."

"No," said Ava. "I don't know. Let's go find out."

"Nope," said Emma. "Still not happening. I'm just going to wait here until you chicken out."

"Oh okay," said Ava. "That's fine. Have fun waiting alone inside a graveyard."

Emma looked around. "Oh no, are we seriously in the graveyard?" The fog covered everything. She reached out and touched the freezing metal gate to the graveyard. It squeaked closed and latched with a PANG.

"Ava?" Emma looked around. "Ava? I can't see anything. It's super scary, just like you thought it would be."

Emma walked toward something glowing.

"Ava? Hey, where did you go? I think I'm going to pee my pants."

Emma reached her hand out. "I'm sorry to be such a wuss. Can I take your hand please?"

She stumbled against a gravestone, then found a protruding arm. She grabbed the hand, stumbling on some loose dirt.

"Oh, there you are," said Emma. "It's so dark I literally can't even see my shoulders." She chuckled. "Be careful of the gravestones, I almost tripped over this one."

Emma followed, walking carefully through the stones.

"You're right, Ava," she said. "We should probably be quiet. I don't really believe in ghosts or anything, but still. It's a graveyard."

She kept walking slowly through the night. The mist cleared a little at the other edge of the graveyard.

Emma could see the gravestones. She realized she was actually leading the way now. "Hey," she said. It's pretty clear up here, come on!"

She stepped ahead and the hand pulled away.

"Who are you talking to?" said Ava.

Emma turned around.

Ava stood outside the metal gate, resting her palms on the painted black spears at the top. "You were right," she said. "I got super scared and ran straight through the middle. I waited around just in case you came through here, too."

Emma looked down at her hand.

It was freezing cold.

Little black streaks were burned into her palm, in the shape of finger bones. She looked back into the mist. Her heart started racing.

"Are you okay?" Ava let go of the gate and walked around to open it.

Emma grabbed her stained hand with her other hand.

Ava rushed in and looked at her friend.

Emma's eyes were wide open. Her breathing was crazy fast. She pulled at her jacket sleeve. The dark streaks spread from her hand, up her wrist.

She pulled harder. The streaks spread up her wrist to her forearm.

"What happened?" Ava asked. "Are you okay? What's going on?"

Emma tore off the jacket completely, throwing it down to the ground.

Ava reached for Emma's hand.

"No!" hissed Emma. "Don't – touch – me."

Ava pulled her hand away. "You're freaking me out, Emma. Why is your hand all black?"

"Why is your neck so tasty?" Emma grabbed Ava's shoulders and pulled her in close for a big hug.

17 – LIPS SEALED

Sarah Parrish loved to earn 'A's on her tests, she would set them in a stack of 3-ring plastic binding, zipped in her trapper-keeper. She loved to sit with her friends at lunch and talk about who was wearing the cutest clothes, who styled their hair the nicest, and which boy had suddenly become cute.

But above all, Sarah loved to heckle Zane, the freshman who transferred to Decatur High School last year from somewhere down South in the bayou. "Why did you leave your swamp?" was the first thing she had asked him. "Your parents didn't like you anymore?"

It used to crack her friends up. "His momma was a gator and his daddy was too dumb to know the difference," she would say. They would all walk away laughing and forget all about it. Every time Sarah saw him, she would make her way over to him and crack a new joke.

Zane would flush red every time, smiling and looking down, but he never said anything back. Being a loner, he seemed pretty happy for any attention at all. After a few months of city life, he had started combing his hair and wearing the same clothes as all the other high school boys. You wouldn't be able to tell he wasn't from Decatur unless you already knew.

Despite this, Sarah still felt compelled to go up to him every day. "Why don't you ever talk, swamp rat? They never taught you how, down in the boonies?" Her friends began to think it was less and less funny, and they even stopped laughing politely.

"Why do you hate Zane so bad?" asked her friend Tina, one day. She sipped her chocolate milk through a straw, and looked innocently at Sarah.

Sarah tensed up and glared back at her. "If you like him so much, why don't you go out with him?" she retorted. She crumpled up her mini bag of Doritos with chips still inside it.

The whole table of girls looked over at Zane.

He noticed them and dropped his chin, smiling. After a few moments he stood up and walked over to their table. "Hi," he said, and waved his hand. "Sarah, I just want to say thanks. It's been real hard moving up here, and you've been too kind to always come up and say something."

A few seconds stretched into a long awkward moment as the girls all shifted their weight uncomfortably.

"You're a moron, Zane," Sarah snapped. "I only talk to you because you're an embarrassment to all the other dumb boys that want to act like men. Nobody likes you around here and we all wish you would crawl back to the bayou."

Zane's smile faded, for the first time. "Just because you know how to say all those mean things, don't mean you should," he mumbled. He turned his back on the girls and slunk away slowly.

"Wait," said Tina. Zane spun around to face her. "I agree. And it's not true that nobody likes you around here. I do." She stood up and grabbed her lunch tray, joining him.

"Tina, don't you walk away with that voodoo toad," Sarah called after them. "None of the girls ever liked you anyways." The other girls at the table sat quiet and still, their eyes wide.

Zane turned back to face Sarah. "If you don't have

anything nice to say, don't say anything at all!" he said in a loud enough whisper, they all heard it.

Sarah grabbed her lunch tray and stormed out.

Later that night, Sarah washed her face in her bathroom sink. She dabbed a cotton swab with witch hazel across her eye shadow and mascara. She flipped it over and wiped the cherry-red lipstick from her lips.

Wincing in pain, she dropped the swab and looked in the mirror. Her lips were dry and cracked, and puffier than usual. She gingerly applied some chap stick and made a kissy face, smiling as she turned out the light and pranced to her bed.

In the dark, she looked up at the ceiling. If she didn't have anything nice to say, she shouldn't say anything at all? Life would be so boring without her jokes. All her friends would miss out.

When the sun crept in the curtains the next morning, Sarah stretched her arms and yawned so wide her mouth hurt. She sprang to her feet, running to the mirror. Her lips were covered in small cuts from top to bottom and side to side. She grabbed some cortisone cream and dabbed at the wounds.

Digging through her winter wardrobe in her bedroom, she found a turtleneck and pulled it up over her mouth. She wore it this way the whole day at school.

During lunch, Sarah sat with her friends, but she didn't say a word. Tina was not there. The girls made the usual banter: nice nails, fancy earrings, and a cute new substitute for history. As they talked they huddle closer together, eventually shouldering out Sarah from the group.

Tears welled up in Sarah's eyes. She stood up and slipped away. She passed Tina and Zane, sitting at a table together, too busy laughing to notice her. In the lunchroom doors, Sarah saw her reflection. There was blood on the top of her turtleneck, just outside her mouth.

She hurried to the bathroom. Painfully pulling the sweater down, the blacks of her eyes widened as she beheld a ghastly sight: blood was seeping from her lips where the cracks had grown thicker and deeper.

Sarah grabbed her book bag from her locker and ran home, her hand up to her face the whole way. When she got back, she ran up to her bathroom and poured hydrogen peroxide on a rag. She wiped it across her cuts, cleaning the blood, a white foam bubbling up in its place.

Every time she swiped, little bits of her lip came off until at last, she discovered that under the wound was blank space where her mouth used to be. She tried to open it and felt her teeth and tongue moving inside. "Bbbbbmmm," she tried to say, her words muffled beyond recognition.

Sarah poked a finger against this new cheek below her nose. It was solid. She clawed her whole hand and pulled at the skin, but it was sealed shut.

Sarah started to panic, walking around her house picking up every object she could find. There must be some way to pry open her mouth. She could not tell her parents, because they would make her go to the hospital. She would be on the news for this and everyone would know what a freak she had become.

A great thirst came over her.

Sarah ran to the kitchen. How would she eat and drink?

An idea struck her.

She poured herself a cup of water. She tilted the full glass towards her and stuck her nose in, sucking the water through it. Down into her belly it went, but the need to breathe forced her to pull out and sneeze water and snot all over the kitchen floor.

She breathed in and out through her nose, exasperated. She set down the glass on the counter and ripped off a paper towel. Bending down to wipe up the mess, her hands shook. She saw the ripples of her tears dripping down into the mess.

The phone rang. Sarah finished wiping up the mess as it rang and rang. She looked at the receiver.

It stopped.

Sarah threw the wet paper towel into the trash bin.

The phone rang again. This time, she lifted it off the cradle and set her ear to it.

"Hello, Sarah. I know you there, I can hear you breathing," said the voice on the other line. It was familiar. "This is Zane. My mama told me it wasn't nice to cast a spell on you, so I'm going to give you a second chance."

"Hhbbmmm!" cried Sarah, but the line went dead.

Sarah hung up the phone. She walked to her bathroom and found her makeup kit. Using lipstick and eye liner, she drew a pair of lips where they used to be, on her face.

That night, Sarah skipped dinner. Her mother came in to see if the was feeling well. She put her hand on her forehead in the dim lighting. "I should get the thermometer and take your temperature."

Sarah vigorously shook her head no, and patted her mother's thigh.

"All right, dear. Get some sleep. Hopefully this will pass by morning," her mother said. She got up and turned out the light, closing the door quietly behind her.

Sarah looked at the ceiling for hours, dreading the darkness. From time to time, she would rest her fingers on her chin and run them up to her nose. She could feel her slimy lipstick smear across her face. Eventually, she passed out from exhaustion.

In the morning, Sarah woke with a fright. She clasped her hand to her face. Her lips were back where they should be. She opened her mouth and poked out her tongue. She touched her teeth. Smiling, she jumped out of bed.

Perhaps it had all been just a dream! Sarah looked down at the bed and saw lipstick smeared all over her pillowcase.

At lunchtime that day at school, Sarah saw Zane sitting with Tina as she was making her way to her friends table.

"Hi, Zane. Hi Tina," she said.

Zane and Tina looked up at her apprehensively.

Sarah let go of the breath she had been holding. "I feel really bad about what I said to you both. I'd like to make it up to you two. Would you join us all for lunch?"

"That's awful kind of you, Sarah," said Zane. He winked at her. "We would be delighted."

From that day on, Sarah Parrish tried to find nice things to say about everyone she met.

18 – SCARED TO DEATH

"Vicky, I'm home!" Vicky's mom walked into the house, carrying her groceries. "Did you finish your homework already?"

She walked into the living room. The furniture was tipped over. The computer was missing. There was a note on the living room table.

Vicky's mom dropped her groceries and the eggs popped with a sickening smack! She ran to the table and picked up the note. Her hands trembled.

"If you ever want to see your daughter again..." she read out loud.

"RRAGH!" Two hands popped out from under the table and grabbed Vicky's mom's legs.

"Daaaaahh!" Vicky's mom threw the note up in the air. Her heart beat fast. She fell backwards onto the carpet.

The tablecloth lifted up.

Vicky jumped out. "Boo!" She laughed. "Gotcha, mom."

Vicky's mom cried, gasping for air.

Vicky kicked her mom gently. "Mom, it's just a joke. Get up."

Vicky's mom whispered, "It's not funny, Vicky. You scared me half to death." She reached over and grabbed a tissue, dabbing the black mascara bleeding from her eyes.

She grabbed another tissue and reached for the liquid eggs, seeping into the carpet.

"Well I better not scare you again, so I don't scare

you all the way to death!" Vicky laughed.

Her mom stared at her, silent. "Did you do your homework?"

Vicky looked at the carpet. "No, mom. I was too busy planning your surprise."

Her mom blew snot into the tissue. "I will talk about this with your father when he comes home."

Vicky laughed again, nervously. "If he comes home. Right?"

"Not funny, Vicky." Her mom picked up the groceries and carried them to the kitchen. "Would you mind helping me wash up that egg off the carpet?" she said over her shoulder.

"No thanks, mom!" replied Vicky. "I have homework to do. Besides, you dropped them." She ran upstairs to her room.

That night, her father came up to her room. He knocked on the door, then opened it without waiting for a reply.

"I don't have much time, Vicky, so I'll keep this short." He sat down at her desk and turned the chair to face her.

Vicky sat on her bed, reading a magazine. She turned her back on her dad.

"You can't keep scaring your mom. You have more important things to do, like focus on schoolwork. You're in big trouble, so much trouble I haven't even thought of a consequence yet. I want to be a nice dad, but I can't when you keep causing so much trouble. I'm willing to offer you a deal."

He took out a big garbage bag and started placing Vicky's belongings into it.

"Hey, that's my stuff! What are you doing?" Vicky threw the magazine and rushed at her dad.

Her dad reached the bag away from her. "These are your things that we gave you. I will only give them back when you prove that you're not a bad kid."

Vicky's eyes watered. Her lip trembled. She tried to hide it. "I'm..." her voice faltered.

She tried again. "I'm not a bad kid."

Her dad sighed. "Don't make me do something really awful, like send you off to live with your grammy."

"I like grammy," said Vicky. "At least her breath doesn't stink like coffee and failure."

Her dad pulled up the garbage bag filled with stuff and walked out of the room.

Three days later, Vicky's mom came home from work.

She opened the door. The furniture was in place. Everything was normal. "Vicky?" she called. "I'm home!"

No answer. Vicky's mom carried her groceries to the kitchen. She stopped outside the entryway. Slowly, she peeked around the corner.

Nothing. She chuckled to herself and walked in. She set her groceries on the counter.

A little pool of water was dripping from the fridge. She grabbed the carton of milk and opened the fridge.

"RRAGH!" Vicky jumped out of the fridge.

Her mom fell backwards and hit her head on the counter.

The milk hit the ground and the carton splashed open.

"Mom, you should clean up that milk!" Vicky laughed.

Her mom was still and silent.

The milk dribbled out of the carton, spreading across the floor.

"Mom," said Vicky. She laughed. "I'm not falling for that. You're going to try to scare me? Huh?" Vicky closed the fridge door and sat looking at her mom. She poked her.

Her mom didn't move.

Vicky pinched her mom's nose.

Her mom didn't move.

Vicky's blood prickled. "Mom?"

She shook her mom and slapped her face.

Her mom didn't move.

Vicky stood up and grabbed her mom's purse from the counter. She shook it out and found her cell phone. She picked it up and unlocked it with her mom's password.

"No!" she cried. "I'm going to be in so much trouble!"

Vicky threw the phone down and shook her hands. She leaned down and put her face next to her mom's face. "MOM!" she screamed.

Her mom didn't move.

Vicky ran outside. She looked around. The shovel was leaning up against the fence.

She grabbed the shovel and dug in the garden. She heaved up a big pile of dirt.

She kept digging until her fingers were blistered and blood ran down her wrists.

She ran inside and grabbed her mom by the shoulders.

With the last of her strength, she dragged her mom out to the garden, her feet thumping each step on the way down.

"I'm so sorry, mom!" said Vicky. She kissed her mom's cheek. "I love you. I didn't mean to scare you to death."

She gently pushed her mom into the hole in the garden. Then she covered her up with dirt.

Vicky ran inside and and threw away the groceries. She threw away her mom's purse and phone.

Then she ran upstairs to do homework.

Later, Vicky's dad came home.

Vicky ran downstairs.

Her dad smiled. "Hello, Vicky! Did you have a good day?"

Vicky shivered. Cold sweat trickled down her sides. "It was okay," she said. "I finished my homework."

She walked up to her dad and hugged him. "Dad, I've been doing a lot of thinking," she said. "I have been a bad kid. Very bad. And I'm sorry. I want to act better and be nicer to you and mom."

"Thanks, sweetie. I know I can overreact when I'm upset. Actually, I put all your stuff back up in your room. I set it all in your closet." He looked around. "Hey, where is mom?"

Vicky's eyes went wide. "I don't know." she lied. "She hasn't come home yet."

"That's odd," said her dad. "Well let me check."

Vicky's dad took out his phone. He tapped the screen.

A muffled ring tone came from the kitchen. Music played softly.

Vicky looked at her dad.

Her dad walked into the kitchen. The music was coming from the trashcan.

He put his hand on the lid of the trashcan. Vicky ran forward to stop him.

"Oh hello," said Vicky's mom. "Were you two looking for me?"

Vicky shivered and turned around.

Her mom was standing there in a bath towel. Her hair was dripping wet.

Vicky backed away and moved behind her dad.

"Hi, Honey!" Vicky's dad walked forward and kissed her mom. "That's so weird, I thought I heard your phone in the trash can."

Vicky's mom laughed. "Well it's been a crazy day. I stopped to help with this incident on the way home. The groceries went bad so I threw them away. I must have accidentally dropped my purse in there too."

"Oh no," Vicky's dad have her mom a big hug. "You look like you're a bit shaken. What happened?"

Vicky looked away from them. She stepped back until she was pressed against the kitchen counter.

"I can't tell you all the details in front of Vicky," said her mom. "It was pretty bad. The worst part is the family that's going to suffer."

Vicky's mom walked toward Vicky. "But at least we're all here safe and sound, right?"

Vicky looked up at her mom. She still had some dirt clinging to the roots of her hair. Everything was normal except for one thing. He eye color was gone. Inside the whites of her eyes were two black lumps, staring into her.

"I love you two very much," said her mom. "And I won't let anything tear this family apart."

She leaned in and hugged Vicky. Her arms and face were as cold as a basement. Her wet hair wrapped around Vicky's back and dripped dirt onto her skin.

BE WARNED

If you have read this book and find that strange things are occurring in your life, it could be from the deep, dark magic that these stories have brought about. The only cure is to go out and find all the other titles written by this storyteller.

Buy them. Review them. Support your storyteller and break the curse!

Other titles include:

Karate vs. Ninjas – Book 1: Origins
Karate vs. Ninjas – Book 2: Shadow of the Ninja
Corrine Wants to Grow Up
Corrine Wants to Grow Up: the Coloring Book

ABOUT THE AUTHOR

Jules Danger Fox is an author and illustrator from a small island in the most remote inhabited location on earth. He likes to write children's stories because it's fun, and you should do what you love doing.

He travels the world with his wife and daughter seeking adventure, intrigue and gluten-free pizza. You can find out more about his other titles, as well as up and coming projects here: (go snoop, there's plenty of dirt.)

www.julesdangerfox.com
www.facebook.com/julesfoxauthor
@julesdangerfox on twitter and instagram

Made in the USA
Las Vegas, NV
27 October 2021

33158632R00075